THEN OF A SUDDEN THEY MADE FOR EACH OTHER

# In The Court

## of

# King Arthur

# In the Court
## of
# King Arthur

By
**Samuel E. Lowe**

*Illustrations by*
**Neil O'Keeffe**

**WHITMAN PUBLISHING CO.**
RACINE - WISCONSIN

# Table of Contents

# Who Was King Arthur?

KING ARTHUR, who held sway in Camelot with his Knights of the Round Table, was supposedly a king of Britain hundreds of years ago. Most of the stories about him are probably not historically true, but there was perhaps a real king named Arthur, or with a name very much like Arthur, who ruled somewhere in the island of Britain about the sixth century.

Among the romantic spires and towers of Camelot, King Arthur held court with his queen, Guinevere. According to tradition, he received mortal wounds in battling with the invading Saxons, and was carried magically to fairyland to be brought back to health and life. Excalibur was the name of King Arthur's sword—in fact, it was the name of two of his swords. One of these tremendous weapons Arthur pulled from the stone in which it was imbedded, after all other knights had failed. This showed that Arthur was the proper king. The other Excalibur was given to Arthur by the Lady of the Lake —she reached her hand above the water, as told in the story, and gave the sword to the king. When Arthur was dying, he sent one of his Knights of the Round Table, Sir Bedivere, to throw the sword back into the lake from which he had received it.

The Knights of the Round Table were so called because they customarily sat about a huge marble table, circular in shape. Some say that thirteen knights could sit around that table; others say that as many as a hundred and fifty could find places there. There sat Sir Galahad, who would one day see the Holy Grail. Sir Gawain was there, nephew of King Arthur. Sir Percivale, too, was to see the Holy Grail. Sir Lancelot—Lancelot of the Lake, who was raised by that same Lady of the Lake who gave Arthur his sword—was the most famous of the Knights of the Round Table. He loved Queen Guinevere.

All the knights were sworn to uphold the laws of chivalry—to go to the aid of anyone in distress, to protect women and children, to fight honorably, to be pious and loyal to their king.

# In the Court of King Arthur

# In the Court
## of
# King Arthur

CHAPTER ONE

## Allan Finds a Champion

"I CANNOT carry your message, Sir Knight."
Quiet-spoken was the lad, though his heart held a moment's fear as, scowling and menacing, the knight who sat so easily the large horse, flamed fury at his refusal.

"And why can you not?  It is no idle play, boy, to flaunt Sir Pellimore.  Brave knights have found the truth of this at bitter cost."

"Nevertheless, Sir Knight, you must reeds find another

message bearer. I am page to Sir Percival and he would
deem it no service to him should I bear a strange knight's
message."

"Then, by my faith, you shall learn your lesson. Since
you are but a youth it would prove but poor sport to thrust
my sword through your worthless body. Yet shall I find Sir
Percival and make him pay for the boorishness of his page.
In the meantime, take you this."

With a sweep the speaker brought the flat side of his
sword down. But, if perchance, he thought that the boy would
await the blow he found surprise for that worthy skillfully
evaded the weapon's downward thrust.

Now then was Sir Pellimore doubly wroth.

"Od's zounds, and you need a trouncing. And so shall
I give it you, else my dignity would not hold its place." Suit-
ing action to word the knight reared his horse, prepared to bring
the boy to earth.

It might have gone ill with Allan but for the appearance
at the turn of the road of another figure—also on horseback.
The new knight perceiving trouble, rode forward.

[16]

"What do we see here?" he questioned. "Sir Knight, whose name I do not know, it seems to me that you are in poor business to quarrel with so youthful a foe. What say you?"

"As to with whom I quarrel is no concern of anyone but myself. I can, however, to suit the purpose, change my foe. Such trouncing as I wish to give this lad I can easily give to you, Sir Knight, and you wish it?"

"You can do no more than try. It may not be so easy as your boasting would seeming indicate. Lad," and the new-comer turned to the boy, "why does this arrogant knight wish you harm?"

"He would have me carry a message, a challenge to Sir Kay, and that I cannot do, for even now I bear a message from Sir Percival, whose page I am but yesterday become. And I must hold true to my own lord and liege."

"True words and well spoken. And so for you, Sir Knight of the arrogant tongue, I hope your weapon speaks equally well. Prepare you, sir."

Sir Pellimore laughed loudly and disdainfully.

"I call this great fortune which brings me battle with

you, sir, who are unknown but who I hope, none the less, are a true and brave knight."

The next second the two horses crashed together. Sir Pellimore soon proved his skill. The Unknown, equally at ease, contented himself with meeting onslaught after onslaught, parrying clever thrusts and wicked blows. So they battled for many an hour.

Allan, the boy, with eyes glistening, waited to see the outcome of the brave fight. The Unknown, his champion, perhaps would need his aid through some dire misfortune and he was prepared.

Now the Unknown changed his method from one of defense to one of offense. But Sir Pellimore was none the less skillful. The third charge of his foe he met so skillfully that both horses crashed to the ground. On foot, the two men then fought—well and long. Until, through inadvertence, the Unknown's foot slipped and the next moment found his shield splintered and sword broken.

"Now then, by my guardian saint, you are truly vanquished," Sir Pellimore exclaimed exultantly. "Say you so?"

But the Unknown had already hurled himself, weapon-

less, upon the seeming victor and seizing him about the waist with mighty strength, hurled him to the ground. And even as the fallen knight, much shaken, prepared to arise, lo, Merlin the Wizard appeared and cast him into a deep sleep.

"Sire," the Wizard declared, "do you indeed run many dangers that thy station should not warrant. And yet, I know not whether we, your loyal subjects, would have it otherwise."

Now Allan, the boy, realized he was in the presence of the great King. He threw himself upon his knees.

"Rise lad," said King Arthur kindly. "Sir Percival is indeed fortunate to have a page, who while so young, yet is so loyal. So shall we see you again. Kind Merlin," and the King turned to the Wizard, "awaken you this sleeping knight whose only sin seems an undue amount of surliness and arrogance, which his bravery and strength more than offset."

Now Sir Pellimore rubbed his eyes. "Where am I?" he muttered drowsily. Then as realization came, he sprang to his feet.

"Know you then, Sir Pellimore," said Merlin, "he with whom you fought is none other than Arthur, the King."

The knight stood motionless, dumbfounded. But only for a moment.

"If so, then am I prepared for such punishment as may come. But be it what it may, I can say this, that none with whom I fought has had more skill or has shown greater bravery and chivalry. And more than that none can say."

And the knight bowed low his head, humbly and yet with a touch of pride.

"Thou art a brave knight, Sir Pellimore. And to us it seems, that aside from a hasty temper, thou couldst well honor us by joining the Knights of the Round Table. What saith thou?"

"That shall I gladly do. And here and now I pledge my loyalty to none other than Arthur, King of Britain, and to my fellow knights. And as for you, boy, I say it now—that my harsh tongue and temper ill became the true knight I claim to be."

"Brave words, Sir Pellimore," said the King. "So let us back to the castle. We see that Merlin is already ill at ease."

## CHAPTER Two

# Allan Goes Forth

SO THEN the four, the good King, Sir Pellimore, Merlin the Wizard, and Allan, page to Sir Percival, came to the great castle of Britain's king.

Arthur led them into the great hall in which were placed many small tables and in the center of them all was one of exceeding size and round. Here was to be found a place for Sir Pellimore but though the King searched long, few seats did he find which were not bespoken. Yet finally he found one which did well for the new arrival.

"Here then shall you find your place at the Round Table, good knight," said the King. "And we trust that you will bring renown and honor to your fellowship, succor to those who are in need and that always will you show true chivalry. And we doubt not but you will do all of these."

Sir Pellimore bowed low his head nor did he make reply because within him surged a great feeling of gratitude.

The King turned away and Merlin followed him to the

upraised dais. So now the two seated themselves and joined in earnest talk.

At the door, Allan had waited, for he would not depart until His Majesty had seated himself. A strange gladness was in the boy's heart, for had not his King fought for him? Here in this court, he too would find adventure. Sir Percival mayhap, some day, would dub him knight, should he prove faithful and worthy. What greater glory could there be than to fight for such a King and with such brave men?

"But I must be off," he suddenly bethought himself, "else Sir Percival will not be pleased." And therewith, he made great haste to depart.

"Aye, sire," Merlin was now speaking, "my dream is indeed weighted with importance. But by the same taken, it cannot be known until you call your court together so that it may be heard by all."

"Then mean you, kind Merlin, that we must call not only those of the Round Table but all other knights and even pages and squires?"

"Even so, sire. And yet, since Whitsunday is but a few

days away, that should be no hard matter. For the knights of your court, except Sir Launcelot and Sir Gawaine are here, prepared for such tourneys and feasts fit to celebrate that day."

"So then shall it be. Even now our heralds shall announce that we crave the attendance of all those who pledge loyalty to our court. For I know well that they must be of no mean import, these things we shall hear. We pray only that they shall be for our good fortune."

The Wizard, making no reply, bent low and kissed his King's hand. Then he departed.

Came now his herald whom the King had summoned.

"See to it that our court assembles this time tomorrow. Make far and distant outcry so that all who are within ear may hear and so hurry to our call. And mark you this well. We would have Sir Launcelot and our own nephew, Sir Gawaine, present even though they departed this early morn for Cornwall. See you to it."

Swiftly the herald made for the door to carry out the commands of his King. But even as he reached it, Arthur called again to him.

"We have a fancy, good herald, we fain would have you follow. Ask then Sir Percival to let us have the services of his page who seems a likely youth and bid this youth go hence after the two absent knights, Sir Gawaine and Sir Launcelot and give to them our message, beseeching their return. Tell not the boy it is we who have asked that he go."

"It shall be done as you will, sire," replied the herald. No surprise did he show at the strangeness of the King's command for long had he been in his service and well he knew the King's strange fancies.

Sir Percival gave ready consent, when found. So when the boy had returned from the errand forespoken, the herald announced that he must hasten after the two knights and bid them return.

"And by my faith, lad, you have but little time and you must speed well. For tomorrow at this time is this conclave called, and the two knights are already many miles on their journey. Take you this horse and hasten."

Then, as the eager youth, quick pulsed, made haste to obey, the herald added in kindly voice:

"It would be well could you succeed, lad. For it is often true that through such missions, newcomers prove future worthiness for knighthood."

"I thank you greatly for your kindness," replied the boy. "I can but try to the uttermost. No rest shall I have until I meet with the two knights."

So now Allan sought out and bespoke his own lord.

"I wish you well, Allan," said Sir Percival. "And say you to my friends Launcelot and Gawaine should they prove reluctant that they will favor their comrade, Sir Percival, if they would make haste and hurry their return. Stop not to pick quarrel nor to heed any call, urgent though it may seem. Prove my true page and worthy."

"I shall do my very best, my lord. And, this my first commission, shall prove successful even though to make it so, I perish."

Swiftly now rode forth the boyish figure. Well, too, had Arthur chosen. Came a day when, than Allan, no braver, truer knight there was. But of that anon.

## CHAPTER THREE

# A Combat

"GOOD Launcelot, I trust that good fortune shall be with us and that our adventures be many and the knights we meet bold and brave."

"Of that, Gawaine, we need have no fear. For adventure ever follows where one seeks and often enough overtakes the seeker. Let us rather hope that we shall find Sir Tristram and Sir Dinadian, both of Cornwall. For myself I would joust with Sir Tristram than whom braver and bolder knight does not live."

"And as for me," spoke Gawaine, "my anxiety is to see Mark, the king of Cornwall, and tell him to his face that I deem him a scurvy hound since he promised protection to Beatrice of Banisar as she passed through his lands and yet broke his promise and so holds her for ransom."

"And there shall I help you, dear Gawaine. For bitterly shall Mark rue his unknightly act. Shall I even wait for my event with Sir Tristram until your business is done."

"Aye, and gladly will Sir Tristram wait, I wot, if he deems it honor to meet with Sir Launcelot du Lake. For no knight there is who doth not know of your prowess and repute, Sir Tristram least of all."

"Kind words, Gawaine, for which I thank you. Yet, if I mistake not, yonder, adventure seems to wait. And we but a little more than two score miles from our gates."

Ahead of them and barring their way were ten knights. Launcelot and Gawaine stopped not a moment their pace but rode boldly forward.

"And wherefor do you, strange Knights, dispute our passage?" asked Sir Gawaine.

"Safely may you both pass unless you be gentlemen of King Arthur's court," quote the leader who stepped forward to answer.

"And what if we be, Sir Knight?" replied Sir Launcelot mildly.

"And if you be then must you battle to the uttermost. For we owe loyalty to King Ryence who is enemy of King Arthur. Therefore, are we his enemies too, and enemies also

[27]

of all of King Arthur's subjects. And thus, we flaunt our enmity. We here and now call King Arthur an upstart and if you be of his court you cannot do aught else but fight with us."

"Keep you your words," said Sir Gawaine, "until we have ceased our quarrel. Then if you will you may call Arthur any names. Prepare you."

Boldly Sir Launcelot and Sir Gawaine charged upon the foe. Nor did the knights who met them know who these two were, else milder were their tone. Such was the valor of the two and such their strength that four men were thrown from their horses in that first attack and of these two were grievously wounded.

Together and well they fought. Easily did they withstand the men of King Ryence. Four men were slain by their might, through wondrous and fearful strokes, and four were sorely wounded. There lay the four against an oaken tree where they had been placed in a moment's lull. But two knights were left to oppose Launcelot and Gawaine but these two were gallant men and worthy, the very best of all the ten.

So they fought again each with a single foe. Hard pressed were the two men of King Ryence, yet stubbornly

they would not give way. And as each side gave blow for blow, so each called "for Arthur" or "for Ryence," whichever the case might be. Many hours they fought until at last Sir Launcelot by a powerful blow crashed both foe and foe's horse to the ground.

And as the other would further combat, though exceedingly weak, Sir Launcelot, upraised lance in hand by a swift stroke smote sword from out of his weakened grasp.

"Thou art a brave knight, friend. And having fought so well, I ask no further penance but this, that you do now declare King Arthur no upstart. I care not for your enmity but I will abide no slander."

"So must I then declare, since you have proven better man than I," declared the conquered knight. "And for your leniency I owe you thanks. Wherefore then to whom am I grateful? I pray your name?"

"That I shall not tell until I hear your own," replied Launcelot.

"I am known as Ronald de Lile," the other replied in subdued tone.

"Truly and well have I heard of you as a brave knight," was the reply, "and now I know it to be so. I am Sir Launcelot du Lake."

"Then indeed is honor mine and glory, too. For honor it is to succumb to Sir Launcelot."

But now both heard the voice of Gawaine. Weak had he grown, but weaker still his foe. Gawaine had brought the other to earth at last with swift and mighty blow and such was the force of his stroke the fallen man could not rise although he made great ado so to do.

"So must I yield," this knight declared. "Now will I admit Arthur no upstart, but though I die for it I do declare no greater king than Ryence ever lived."

"By my faith, your words are but such as any knight must hold of his own sovereign prince. I cannot take offense at brave words, Sir Knight. Now, give me your name, for you are strong and worthy."

"I am Marvin, brother of him who fought with your comrade. And never have we met bolder and greater knights."

"I am Gawaine and he who fought your brother is none other than Launcelot."

"Then truly have we met no mean foes," replied the other.

Conquered and conquerers now turned to make the wounded as comfortable as they well could be. After which, our two knights debated going on their journey or tarrying where they were until the morn.

"Let us wend our way until we find fit place for food and rest. There can we tarry." So spoke Launcelot and the other agreed.

Then they took leave of Sir Marvin and Sir Ronald and so on their way. Not many miles did they go however before they found suitable place. Late was the hour and weary and much in need of rest were the two knights. So they slept while, half his journey covered, Allan sped onward, making fast time because he was but light of weight and his horse exceeding swift.

## CHAPTER FOUR

# Allan Meets the Knights

FROM the first day when Allan began to understand the tales of chivalry and knightly deeds, he fancied and longed for the day when he would grow into manhood and by the same token into knighthood. Then would he go unto King Arthur on some Pentecost and crave the boon of serving him. Mayhap, too, he would through brave and worthy deeds gain seat among those of the Round Table. So he would dream, this youth with eager eyes, and his father, Sir Gaunt, soon came to know of his son's fancies and was overly proud and pleased with them. For he himself had, in his days, been a great and worthy knight, of many adventures and victor of many an onslaught. It pleased him that son of his would follow in his footsteps.

When Allan was fourteen, Sir Gaunt proceeded to Sir Percival who was great friend of his and bespoke for his son the place of page. And so to please Sir Gaunt and for friend-

ship's sake, Sir Percival gave ready consent. Therewith, he found the youth pleasing to the eye and of a great willingness to serve.

So must we return to Allan who is now on his way for many an hour. As he made his way, he marveled that he should have had notice brought upon himself, for he was young and diffident and should by every token have escaped attention in these his first days at court. How would his heart have grown tumultuous had he known that none other than Arthur himself had made him choice. But that he was not to know for many a year.

Night came on and the boy traveled far. Yet gave he no thought to rest for he knew that he could ill afford to tarry and that only with the best of fortune could he overtake the two knights in time to make early return. About him the woods were dark and mysterious. Owls hooted now and then and other sounds of the night there were, yet was the boy so filled with urge of his mission that he found not time to think of ghosts nor black magic.

Then, as he turned the road he saw the dim shadow of a horse. Ghostly it seemed, until through closer view it

proved flesh and blood. Lying close by was a knight who seemed exceeding weak and sorely wounded.

Quick from his horse came Allan and so made the strange knight be of greater comfort.

Now the knight spoke weakly.

"Grievously have I been dealt with by an outlaw band. This day was I to meet my two brothers Sir Ronald and Sir Marvin yet cannot proceed for very weakness. Which way do you go, lad?"

"I keep on my way to Cornwall," replied Allan.

"From yonder do my brothers journey and should you meet with them bid them hasten here so that together we can go forth to find this outlaw band and it chastise."

"That shall I do, Sir Knight. It grieves me that I may not stay and give you such aid as I may but so must I hasten that I cannot. Yet shall I stop at first abode and commission them to hurry here to you."

"For that I thank you, lad. And should time ever come when you my aid require, know then to call on Philip of Gile."

So Allan pressed forward. At early dawn he came upon Sir Ronald and Sir Marvin who had found rest along the wayside. And when he found that these were the two knights he gave them their brother's message.

"Then must we hasten thence, Ronald. And thank you, lad, for bringing us this message. Choose you and you can rest awhile and partake of such food that we have."

"Of food I will have, Sir Knights, for hunger calls most urgently. But tarry I cannot for I must find Sir Launcelot and Sir Gawaine. Mayhap you have met with them?"

"Of a truth can we say that we have met with them and suffered thereby. Yet do we hold proof as to their knightly valor and skill. They have gone but a little way, for it was their purpose to find rest nearby. We doubt not you will find them at the first fair abode. In the meantime must we hasten to our brother's aid and leave our wounded comrades to such care as they may get."

The knights spoke truly, for Allan found upon inquiry that the two he sought were lodged close by. Boldly the boy called, now for Sir Launcelot, now for Sir Gawaine, but both were overtired and of a great weariness and it took many minutes before at last Sir Launcelot opened wide his eyes.

"And who are you, boy?" for he knew him not.

"My name is Allan and I am page to Sir Percival."

"Come you with a message from Sir Percival? Does he need our help?"

"Nay, sir. Rather do I come with a message from the court—the herald of which sent me urging you and Sir Gawaine to return before sundown for a great conclave is to gather which the King himself has called."

"Awaken then, thou sleepy knight," Sir Launcelot called to his comrade who had not stirred. "It were pity that all this must be told to you again."

Sir Gawaine now arose rubbing eyes still filled with sleep. To him Allan repeated his message.

"What say you, Gawaine? Shall we return?

"As for me," replied Sir Gawaine, "I would say no. What matter if we are or are not present. Already we are late for our present journey's purpose. So say I, let us not return but rather ask this youth to bespeak for us the king's clemency."

"And I, too, am of the same mind, Gawaine. So lad," Sir Launcelot turned to the boy and spoke kindly, "return

you to court and give them our message. This errand on which we are at present bound holds urgent need, else would we return at our King's behest."

Rueful and with a great gloom Allan saw his errand fail.

"Kind sirs, Sir Percival bid me bespeak for him as well, and ask you, as true comrades, to make certain to return. Furthermore, my knights, this, my first mission would be unfortunate if it did not terminate successfully. So I pray you that you return."

Loud and long Sir Launcelot laughed and yet not unkindly while Sir Gawaine placed hand upon the boy's shoulder approvingly.

"By my faith, Launcelot, we can do no more than return. That Percival speaks counts for much, but this youth's honor is also at stake." The light of laughter played in the speaker's eyes.

"Yes," said Sir Launcelot, "let us return. It would be pity to send this lad back after his long journey, without success. So then to our horses and let us make haste. The hours are few and the miles many."

## CHAPTER FIVE

# Merlin's Message

NOW as the sun, a flaming golden ball about which played the wondrous softer colors of filmy clouds, began sinking in the western horizon, the heralds announced everywhere that the time for assemblage had come. Of those few who were not present, chiefest were Sir Launcelot and Sir Gawaine. And for these two the herald of King Arthur was searching the road in vain.

"Think you, Sir Percival, these two will come?" the herald, anxious of tone, inquired. "Our King would have them present and I fancy not the making of excuse for their not appearing."

"It is hard telling, Sir Herald. Far had the page to go and he is young. Then too, it is a question whether should he meet with them, these two have a mind to appear. For I know that their journey to Cornwall is urgent."

Now the knights entered and found place. Then followed the pages, squires and after them such yeoman and varlets as could find room. After each had found his place,

came King Arthur leading his queen. And as they entered, up rose the knights, their vassals, all that were within the hall and raised a mighty shout.

"St. George and Merrie England. Long live King Arthur. Long live Queen Guenever."

Then turned the King toward his loyal subjects and though his lips were seen to move, none heard him for the clamor. So King Arthur turned to seat his queen and then he himself sat down upon his throne, high on the dais.

Then soon after even as bell tolled the hour, Arthur arose. No sign had yet come of Launcelot and Gawaine. So now the herald slipped to the door to cast again a hurried glance for perchance that they might be within vision. And as he went noiselessly, so, too, a quiet fell that the King's words might be heard. But now disturbing this quiet came a great clattering. Arthur turned his eyes, frowning, at the sudden noise. Yet came a greater turmoil, approaching horse's hoofs were heard and then into the great hall thundered the steeds carrying the noble figures of Launcelot and Gawaine. followed but a pace behind by Allan the page.

Straight to the dais they came, the two knights. Allan, however, turned, made hasty exit because he felt himself abashed to be observed by so many eyes. On foot he entered

once again and found place far in the rear where few could observe him.

The two knights now dismounted and knelt before their King.

"We pray your pardon for the lateness of our coming. Yet did we hasten and could not have come the sooner."

"That we feel is so, Sir Knights, for we know you well enough. Nor are we wroth, since come you did. But where, pray, is the message bearer? Truly his speed was great to have reached you in time for your return. And if I mistake not," added the King with great shrewdness, "neither you, Gawaine, nor you Launcelot, were any too ready to return. How then, did the lad urge you?"

"You speak truly, sire," replied Gawaine. "For our errand had need of urgent haste and we were loth to give it up. Yet did the boy urge us and chiefest urge of all to us was where he claimed his own honor demanded the success of his mission. Those were fine words, so did we therefore return."

"Fine words, indeed. Where then is this page? Will you, Sir Herald, bring him forth?"

So Allan came forward, red of face and hating such womanness that would let him blush before all these great men. Knelt he before his King.

"Thou art a good lad and will bear watching. Go thy

way and remember that the road ahead for those who wish to be knights of high nobility is steep and arduous but well worth the trials. Remember too, that this day, Britain's King, said that some day thou wilt prove a worthy and brave knight."

And as Allan with flaming cheeks and glorious pride went to his place far in the rear of the hall the King turned to the assemblage.

"Merlin is here but departs from us tomorrow for many a day. He has had a great dream which affects this court and us and which must be told to all of you. So he has asked us to call you and this we have done. Stand up now Merlin, wisest of men and truest of counselors. Speak."

Up rose Merlin and for wonder as to what his dream might be all held their breath.

"But the other night came Joseph of Armathea to me while I slept. And he chided me that in all Britain so few of all the true and brave knights had thought to seek the wondrous Holy Grail which once was pride of all England.

"And methought I heard him say, 'Truly do I misdoubt the valor of these knights who seek adventure and glory.'

"'Yet,' said I, 'doubt not their valor for can I give surety for it. For Holy Grail, every varlet, let alone those of true blood, would give his life and count it more than worthy.'

[41]

" 'So shall it be!' replied Sir Joseph. 'For the Holy Grail will be found. Whether knight or varlet shall the finder be, I will not say. But this I tell you now. He who finds it shall be pure of heart and noble beyond all men. From whence he cometh, who he is, I will not say. Remember this, Merlin, brave and noble knights there are now in England, brave knights shall come, and some shall come as strangely as shall the Grail. Many deeds will be done that will bring truest of glory to England's name. And never again shall more noble or more worthy knights hold Britain's banner so high. For they who seek the Holy Grail must be worthy even of the search.

" 'Let your King beware that he listen's well to all who come to his court on every Pentecost. And though they who search may not be overstrong, yet while they seek it they will find in themselves many men's strength.'

"And then he left me. But even after he was gone I dreamt on. And I say to you, oh men of England, go you forth and seek this Holy Grail, if within you, you know that you are pure of heart and noble. If you are not, go then and seek to be purified for that is possible. Only one of you will find the Holy Grail, yet is there great glory in the search. May

he who finds it and all the rest who search for it bring greater fame and worthiness to this our land and to him who is our King."

Now Merlin turned to seat himself. But yet before he found his place every man within the hall stood up prepared to make oath then and there to begin the search. Only two kept still, nor did they move. One was Sir Launcelot, the other the youth Allan.

But quick as they who upstood, Merlin spoke again. And though his voice was low, yet was it heard throughout the hall.

"Pledge not yourself today, nor yet tomorrow. Go you hence, first. In your innermost heart find answer to this question. Am I pure, am I worthy for the search? For that you must be before any pledge suffices."

Silent and thoughtful the men found each his seat. And when all had been seated, Arthur, King, arose.

"Wouldst that I felt myself worthy. Yet from this day shall I strive to the uttermost for the time when I shall feel that I am."

And throughout the hall came answering vows: "So shall we all." Within his heart, Allan, the youth, felt a strange radiancy, as he too made this vow, "So shall I."

## Chapter Six

# Yosalinde

NOW came Pentecost and brought with it to King Arthur's Tournament brave knights from everywhere. Distant Normandy, the far shores of Ireland, sent each the flower of its knighthood. Scotland's king was there, the brave Cadoris, to answer the challenge of the King of Northgalis who was also present. Ban, King of Northumberland, had come. Sir Palomides came too, and it was he who was declared, by many to be the bravest and the most skillful of all of Britain's knights. Yet there were equal number and more who held the same for both Sir Launcelot and for Sir Tristram. Sir Lauvecor, leading a hundred knights, came late, with the blessing of his father, who was none other than King of Ireland.

A brave show they all made, these many knights seeking adventure, and each, as he so easily bestrode his steed, found it hard matter to find comrade and friend, for the many who were there. Gay were the colors each knight wore and on some fortune had smiled, for these carried token of some fair lady. Of fair ladies there were many to watch the deeds of skill and

bravery and most beautiful of them all, was Arthur's queen, Guenever.

Sir Launcelot and Sir Gawaine had found no need to journey to Cornwall. For word had come that Sir Tristram had had a bitter quarrel with King Mark and had left his court carrying that wicked King's curse. Tristram had made final demand on the traitorous King to release the maiden Beatrice whom he was holding for ransom and this the King had had no mind to do. Then had the bold knight himself made for the door of the great dungeon and with hilt of sword knocked long and loud to summon the keeper. And when the door was opened this same keeper could not withstay him, nor would he. Then had Tristram carried the maiden to point of safety and so earned her gratitude. Nor would any knight of King Mark take issue with him for none felt the King's deed to be knightly. And though the King made pretense of bearing no ill will, yet did Sir Tristram leave Cornwall that same day.

And Sir Gawaine knew not whether to be pleased or otherwise at the news.

"I would have fancied making rescue of the Lady Beatrice myself. And fancied even more to have told King

Mark the scurvy knave I deem him; yet I doubt not Sir Tristram did the deed well and since it leaves me free to stay and have part in the jousting, I am not displeased."

"And methinks," added Sir Launcelot, "Sir Tristram will make his way hither, for tournament such as this holds all alluring call."

King Arthur, together with Ban of Northumberland, and Sir Percival were declared the judges for all but the last of the three days.

Now then Sir Percival, finding a moment's brief respite, followed by his page rode to the palace where sat his mother and two sisters. There he found Sir Uwaine already in deep converse with Helene, who was the older of the two maidens and whose knight he was.

"See you, son, there do be knights who find time to pay respect to us, even though our own are slower footed." So spoke the Lady Olande yet did it jestingly and with no intent to hurt for she had great love for her son.

"And I doubt not, Uwaine does make up for any seeming lack of mine," replied Sir Percival. "If, mother mine, I were not made a judge, my time would be more my own.

"But here, I must have lost what manners I have been taught. Mother, this is Allan who is my page, and these, Allan, are my sisters Helene and Yosalinde. Allan is son of Sir Gaunt, whom you all know. Forgive my not making you known before this, lad."

Pleasantly did the ladies greet him and so well that he found no embarrassment therewith. And so now Sir Percival turned and spoke in low tones to his mother. Sir Uwaine and his lady walked away, claiming that they must give greeting to certain high ladies. And therewith left Allan, the boy, and Yosalinde, who was even younger than he, to themselves.

Allan strove to speak but found he could not and so sat on horse waiting. The girl calmly watched him from her place, yet was there mischief in her eyes.

"If you would, you may dismount from your horse and find place hither. There is room, as you see," she suggested.

The lad looked uncertain. Yet Sir Percival had already found place next to his mother and was now in earnest converse. So he found he could not do otherwise.

Now Yosalinde laughed at what showed so plainly his unwillingness to sit beside her.

"I shall not bite you. See how harmless I am? No witch, I hope, you think I am. For shame that youth, who would be brave knight, should fear a lady and in especial one so young as I."

"I fear you not," replied Allan hotly.

"Then perhaps you dislike me?" the minx questioned innocently.

"Certes, no. How could I?" the guileless youth replied.

"Then you do like me? Although I doubt I find any pride in that since I must need force the words from you."

At a loss now the lad could not answer. For the girl had better of him because of her quick tongue and he found she twisted his words and meaning to suit her taste. Yet finally, she turned the talk and so Allan found himself telling her of his high hopes. So simply too, without boasting, he told her of the fine words of Arthur to him. And last, because it had made its deep impress upon him, he spoke of Merlin's dream. And of this Yosalinde, now serious and wide eyed, questioned him closely, and soon knew all that he did.

So now Percival uprose and made ready to return to his

duties.  So therefore, too, did Allan, and found he now felt more at ease and without constraint of the girl.

"I *like* you, Allan, and I say it though I should make it harder for you to know, than it was for me.  I give you my friendship and if it help you, take this ring and wear it.  May it serve you in time of stress.  And at all times consider it token of your lady."

And then once again the laughing, teasing minx, she, added:

"Yet, after all, you are but a boy and I am no less a girl. Yet, let us make-believe, you a bold knight and I your lady. Mayhap it may be true some day."

So she was gone now to her mother leaving Allan with stirred feelings and somewhat in a dream, too.  For Sir Percival had to call twice to him before he mounted his own horse. And even as they both made their way, he turned his head back to see if he could perceive aught of this strange girl. And thought he saw a waving hand but was not sure.

## CHAPTER SEVEN

# The Tournament

ON THE first of the three days of the tournament there were great feats of wrestling and trials of archery. So too did yeomen prove their skill with mace and clubs. Foot races were many. And constant flow of ale and food so that none among the yeomen and even of the varlets found aught to want. Many fools there were too and these pleased all mightily.

But as the day advanced of all the yeomen but a half dozen remained for the wrestling. And for each of these but one, there was high acclaim from those other yeomen who were there and from such knights as owed fealty to selfsame banner. And of the archers too, but very few remained for last tests of skill.

For the one yeoman, who wore green tunic and red cap, there was none to cheer. A stranger, he kept silent and yet was equally skillful with the best. He had entered himself for the archery prize and for the wrestling.

"Dost know this knave?" asked King Arthur of Sir Percival.

"Only that he belongs not to any of us of the Round Table," replied Percival.

"Is he forsooth, one of your men, worthy Ban?"

"I would he were, Arthur, yet is he not."

Now Sir Percival rode forward and divided these last six wrestlers into teams. Yet did this man prove victor for he had a wondrous hold which none of the others knew. And when he had won, so turned he to watch and join in the archery. And as he watched came there knaves to him and mocked him.

"Faith though you wrestle well," one spoke, "it doth not make you an archer. For here you find true archery than which none can do better."

"And I carry a club I would fain try on your thick skull," said another who was even less gentle spoken.

"Of a good time, my friend, and you may," replied the lone knave.

"No such time befits the same as now," replied the first knave.

"If they will wait for my trial with bow and arrow I would be the last to keep you waiting." So spoke the stranger.

So then one of the knaves hurried away and received permission.

"Then furnish me a club," said the stranger.

"Here then is mine," offered the third knave.

Yet, forsooth, the club was but a sorry one and so the unknown would not use it.

"Then show you a coward's heart," replied he who would strive with him. And then the three rushed upon the stranger and would do him hurt.

So now came bearing down on the three none other than Allan who had overheard the parley.

"For shame, knaves. No true men would treat stranger so. He asks nothing more than is fair. Give him a club of his choosing."

"Of a faith, young master, this quarrel is none of yours, and warrants no interference. Leave this fellow to us, and we shall give him clubbing of his choosing." And the man who

addressed the boy, though he looked not straight at him, growled surlily.

"I shall give you a thrashing, fool, unless you do my bidding," replied the boy, hotly.

But the three surly brutes moved uneasily. And then came Sir Percival forward.

"What have we here?" he asked.

So Allan waited for the men to say. But they, now frightened, made no spoken word.

"These knaves would play foul tricks on this strange fellow. This one, would strive with him and yet would not offer other club than this. And when the stranger asked to have one of his choice they called him coward and would beat him."

"And I doubt not, fools, this club you offer will not stand one blow." So Sir Percival brought it down on the first knave's head, and, lo, though the blow was not a hard one, yet did the club break in two.

"So methought. Now go you Allan and get club that will do. And then will you, stranger, give this villain a sound

trouncing." And Sir Percival stayed so that the trouble-makers did not depart.

So Allan brought a club which suited the stranger.

Now did the two battle long and well. Both the stranger and he who fought with him were of great strength and each was exceeding quick.

As wood struck wood and each tried to get full blow upon the other, so turned all eyes upon the two. And except for glancing blows neither could bring the other down. And though the sparks flew, yet each held his club and was hardly hurt. So now they rested for a few moments.

And while they waited, the stranger turned to Allan and spoke.

"I thank you for your brave upstanding of me, young master. And I hope some day I may serve you equally well."

"You are a worthy man. Serve me now by trouncing the knave who battles with you."

"I can but try, yet right skillful is the fellow."

So they turned to again. Yet this time the stranger

fought the better. Soon the other was forced back, foot by foot. And even as the stranger seemed to have all the best of it, his foot seeming slipped, and he went to his knees.

Fiercely the other came upon him. Yet as he came closer the stranger's club moved swiftly. From out the seeming victor's hand flew his mighty club and next second found him clubbed to the ground, senseless.

Now the stranger sat himself down for he needed rest sorely. But only for a little while and thereafter he turned to try his skill with bow and arrow. And though he had shown skill in all of the other feats he proved his mastery here. For he was wondrous expert in his archery.

"Here you, is fair target," he finally suggested after many trials. And went to distant tree and removed from bough upon it, all its leaves but one.

"Shoot you all at this. And if you bring it down I will call you skillful."

But only one would try for it. And he came close but missed.

Now did the stranger raise his own bow Nor did he seem

to take aim but let the arrow fly. And the arrow carried the twig and leaf with it to the ground.

"Of a truth," said King Arthur, "a right worthy knave is that and I would speak to him."

So they brought the stranger before the king.

"Thou hast done exceeding well, this day, fellow. Tell us then the banner that you serve."

"That I cannot do. For, sire, such are my master's commands. Yet may I say no knight is more true and worthy."

"Then must we wait for your master's coming. Go thou hence and tell your master he can be proud of thee. And take you this bag of gold besides such other prizes as are yours." So as the knave stood there, the King turned to Sir Dagonet, his jester, who was making himself heard.

"A fool speaks, sire. Yet claim I, like master like man. So then must this fellow's master be right skillful to hold him. And since this master is not you, nor Sir Launcelot, then I pick him to be Sir Tristram."

"Fool's reasoning, yet hath it much sense," said the King.

Now the stranger left. But ere departing, he turned to Allan.

"I trust, young master, I shall see you again. As to who I am, know you for your own keeping—fools ofttimes reason best of all."

The yeoman rode far into the forest. Then when he came to a lone habitation he dismounted. A knight seated near the small window at the further wall greeted him as he entered.

"How did the day turn out? No doubt they trounced you well."

"No, master, no trouncing did I get. Instead, the good King spoke pleasantly unto me, gave me this bag of gold, and commended me to my master. Furthermore, see you these prizes that are mine?"

"Aye," the yeoman continued, not a bit grieved at the knight's banter, "I even heard the King's fool remark that since the man was so good, the master need must be. And then and there he hazarded a shrewd guess that if this master were not the King, nor Sir Launcelot, then it must need be you."

"Then truly am I in good company. Now then tell me what news is there of tomorrow?"

"The King of Northgalis desires your aid. That I heard him say. Sir Launcelot is to joust for Cadoris as is Sir Palomides, and these two, of a truth, make it one-sided."

"Worthy Gouvernail, prove again my faith in you. Procure for me a shield, one that holds no insignia, so that I may enter the lists unbeknownst to any. I would not have them know I am Tristram, so that it may be my good fortune to joust with many knights who know me not."

"That, good master, is not hard. I know a place where I can obtain a black shield, one that holds no other remembrance upon it. It should serve your purpose well."

"By my faith, did ever better knave serve master? Right proud of you am I, Gouvernail. And would that I too had bags of gold I could give you for your loyal service."

"Nay, master, such service as I give I measure not by aught that you can pay."

"That do I know full well, else had you left me long since, for little have I paid," Sir Tristram answered, soft spoken and with great affection.

## CHAPTER EIGHT

# Sir Tristram's Prowess

SO THE next day Sir Tristram, carrying the black shield, went forth to enter the lists. And none knew him. The great conflict had already begun when he arrived. He found himself a place among those knights who jousted for Northgalis And very soon all perceived that this knight with the black shield was skillful and strong. Well and lustily did he battle and none could withstand him. Yet did he not meet with Sir Launcelot nor with Sir Palomides, on this first day. Nor did any know him, but all marveled at his worth and bravery.

So, as the day was done, this Unknown and his servant, Gouvernail, rode back into the forest. And none followed him for he was a brave knight and all respected him and his desire to stay unknown. Yet did the judges declare the side of Northgalis victor and as for single knight, the most worthy was the Unknown. And he was called "the Knight of the Black Shield."

Now as the judges' duties were done, King Arthur showed how wroth he was that strange knight had carried off such great honors.

"Yet do we hope tomorrow shall show other reckoning than this. For good Launcelot shall be there and so shall we."

On the morn the heralds called forth the brave knights once again. And with the call came the "Knight of the Black Shield."

Sir Palomides was await for him, eager and alert, to be the first to joust. And so they, like great hounds, went at each other. And truly, Sir Tristram found his foe a worthy one. Long did they joust without either besting the other until he of the black shield by great skill and fine force brought down a mighty blow and did smite Sir Palomides over his horse's croup. But now as the knight fell King Arthur was there and he rode straight at the unknown knight shouting, "Make thee ready for me!" Then the brave sovereign, with eager heart, rode straight at him and as he came, his horse reared high. And such was the King's strength he unhorsed Sir Tristram.

Now, while the latter was on foot, rode full tilt upon him, Sir Palomides, and would have borne him down but that Sir Tristram was aware of his coming, and so lightly stepping aside, he grasped the arm of the rider and pulled him from his horse. The two dashed against each other on foot and with

their swords battled so well that kings and queens and knights and their ladies stood and beheld them. But finally the Unknown smote his foe three mighty blows so that he fell upon the earth groveling. Then did they all truly wonder at his skill for Sir Palomides was thought by many to be the most skillful knight in Britain.

A knight now brought horse for Sir Tristram, for now, all knew that it must be he. So too was horse brought for Sir Palomides. Great was the latter's ire and he came at Sir Tristram again. Full force, he bore his lance at the other. And so anew they fought. Yet Sir Tristram was the better of the two and soon with great strength he got Sir Palomides by the neck with both hands and so pulled him clean out of his saddle. Then in the presence of them all, and well they marveled at his deed, he rode ten paces carrying the other in this manner and let him fall as he might.

Sir Tristram turned now again and saw King Arthur with naked sword ready for him. The former halted not, but rode straight at the King with his lance. But as he came, the King by wondrous blow sent his weapon flying and for a moment Sir Tristram was stunned. And as he sat there upon his horse the King rained blows upon him and yet did the lat-

ter draw forth his sword and assail the King so hard that he
need must give ground. Then were these two divided by the
great throng. But Sir Tristram, lion hearted, rode here and
there and battled with all who would. And of the knights
who opposed him he was victor of eleven. And all present
marveled at him, at his strength and at his great deeds.

Yet had he not met Sir Launcelot, who elsewhere was
meeting with all who would strive with him. Not many, however, would joust with him for he was known as the very bravest and most skillful. So as he sat there all at ease, there came
the great acclaim for the Knight of the Black Shield. Nor
did Sir Launcelot know him to be Sir Tristram. But he got
his great lance and rushed toward the cry. When he saw
this strange knight he called to him, "Knight of the Black
Shield, prepare for me."

And then came such jousting as had never been seen.
For each knight bowed low his head and came at the other like
the wind. When they met it was very like thunder. Flashed
lance on shields and armor so that sparks flew. And each
would not give to the other one step but by great skill with
shield did avoid the best of each other's blows.

Then did Sir Tristram's lance break in two, and Sir

Launcelot, through further ill fortune, wounded Sir Tristram in his left side. But notwithstanding, the wounded knight brought forth his sword and rushed daringly at the other with a force that Sir Launcelot could not withstand, and gave him a fearful blow. Low in his saddle sagged Sir Launcelot, exceeding weak for many moments. Now Sir Tristram left him so and rode into the forest. And after him followed Gouvernail, his servant.

Sore wounded was Sir Tristram yet made he light of it. Sir Launcelot on his part recovered soon and turned back to the tourney, and thereafter did wondrous deeds and stood off many knights, together and singly.

Now again was the day done and the tournament, too. And to Sir Launcelot was given full honor as victor of the field. But naught would Sir Launcelot have of this. He rode forthwith to his King.

"Sire, it is not I but this knight with the Black Shield who has shown most marvelous skill of all. And so I will not have these prizes for they do not belong to me."

"Well spoken, Sir Launcclot and like thy true self," replied the King. So since this knight is gone, will you go forth with us within the fortnight in search for him. And unless we are in great error we shall find this Knight of the Black Shield no more, no less, than Sir Tristram."

## CHAPTER NINE

# The Kitchen Boy

A MONG all those who came to the court of King Arthur at this Pentecost seeking hospitality, were two strangers in especial, who because of being meanly garbed and of a seeming awkwardness brought forth the mockery and jest of Sir Kay the Seneschal. Nor did Sir Kay mean harm thereby, for he was knight who held no villainy. Yet was his tongue overly sharp and too oft disposed to sting and mock.

Too, the manner of their coming was strange. One was a youth of handsome mien. Despite his ill garb, he seemed of right good worship. Him, our young page Allan found fallen in a swoon, very weak and near unto death, asprawl on the green about a mile from the castle. Thinking that the man was but a villain, he would fain have called one of the men-at-arms to give him aid, but that something drew him to closer view. And then the boy felt certain that this was no villain born for his face bespoke gentle breeding. So he himself hastened for water and by much use of it the man soon opened his eyes and found himself. So he studied the lad as he helped

him to greater ease but either through his great weakness or no desire he did not speak.

"Stranger," said Allan to the man, "if there is aught that I can do for you or if I can help you in any way I give you offer of service. Mayhap of the many knights who are here, there is one whose aid you may justly claim."

The stranger held answer for many moments, then he spoke.

"There are those here, lad, whose service I may well accept for they hold ties of blood to me. But I would not. Rather, if your patience will bear with me, I would fain have your help so that I can appear in the presence of the King this day. For so it is ordained and by appearing there I shall find some part of my vow accomplished. On this holy day, I have boon to ask from your King."

"So shall I and right gladly lead you there. Good sir, my name is Allan. I am page to Sir Percival, and I would bespeak your name."

"I beg of thee, Allan, think not that I am churlish and yet must I withhold my name. For it is part of the vow I have made. Nor, forsooth, am I therefore the less grateful."

"No offense take I, friend. So when you feel disposed I shall guide your steps for audience with our good King."

The stranger, weak and spent, leaning mightily on his young friend made his way to the great hall. And as we have recounted, though all were struck by oddness and meanness of the stranger's clothes, yet only Sir Kay made point to taunt him. Yet did he make no answer to these taunts but waited with a great meekness for his turn before the King. And that he should wait with such meekness was strange for he seemed to be a high born knight.

There were many who sought audience with the King and it was long before the stranger's turn came. Weak he still was, but he made no complaint, and when others would crowd before him so that they could speak the sooner to King Arthur, he did not chide them but permitted it. At last Sir Launcelot came forward, for he had observed this and made each of them find the place which was first theirs, so that the stranger's turn came as it should. Weak though he was he walked with a great firmness to the dais, and none there saw his poor clothes for the fineness of him. The King turned to him and he nodded kindly.

"Speak, friend. In what way can we be of service to thee?"

"Sire," said the stranger, "I come to ask of thee three boons. One I ask this day and on this day one year I shall come before you and crave your favor for the other two."

"If the boon you ask, stranger, is aught we can grant, we shall do so cheerfully, for on this day we heed all prayers."

"I ask very little, sire. This and no more do I wish— that you give me food and drink for one year and that on this day a year hence I shall make my other two prayers."

"It is indeed little you ask. Food and drink we refuse none. It is here. Yet while your petition might well beseem a knave, thou seemeth of right good worship, a likely youth, too, none fairer, and we would fain your prayer had been for horse and armor. Yet may you have your wish. Sir Kay," and the King turned to his Seneschal, "see you to it that this stranger finds his wish satisfied."

So the King turned to others present, for of those who sought audience there were many. And so forgot all of the fair youth for many a day.

Sir Kay laughed mockingly at the unknown.

"Of a truth this is villain born. For only such would ask for food and drink of the King. So therefore he shall find place in our kitchen. He shall help there, he shall have fat broth to satisfy himself and in a year no hog shall be fatter. And we shall know him as the Kitchen Boy."

"Sir Kay," frowned Sir Launcelot, "I pray you cease your mocking. It is not seemly. This stranger, whosoever he may be, has right to make whatsoever request he wishes."

"Nay, Sir Launcelot, of a truth, as he is, so has he asked."

"Yet I like not your mocking," said Sir Launcelot as he looked frowningly at Sir Kay, while next to him stood Sir Gawaine and Sir Percival, neither of whom could scarce contain himself.

"It is well, we know you, Sir Kay. Or, by our guardian saints we would make you answer for your bitter tongue. But that we know it belies a heart of kindness we would long since have found quarrel with you." So spoke Sir Percival and Sir Gawaine nodded in assent.

"Stay not any quarrel for any seeming knowledge of me, kind friends," frowned back Sir Kay.

But the two knights moved away. Sir Kay was of great shame. And so to cover it he turned to the stranger in great fury. "Come then to your kennel, dog," he said.

Out flashed the sword of Sir Gawaine. Yet did Sir Launcelot withhold him.

"Sir, I beg you to do me honor of feasting with us this day?"

"I thank you Sir Launcelot. Yet must I go with Sir Kay and do his bidding. There do be knights well worth their places at the Round Table. And I note right well that they set high example to those who are still but lads and who are to become knights in good time. So to you all I give my thanks."

Then followed the stranger after Sir Kay while the three knights and Allan watched him go and marveled at his meekness.

## Chapter Ten

# Pentecost

AND so in turn came the second stranger before King Arthur. Poorly clothed, too, yet had his coat once been rich cloth of gold. Now it sat most crookedly upon him and was cut in many places so that it but barely hung upon his shoulders.

"Sire," said the stranger, "you are known everywhere as the noblest King in the world. And for that reason I come to you to be made knight."

"Knights, good friend," replied the King, "are not so easily made. Such knights as we do appoint must first prove their worth. We know thee not, stranger, and know not the meaning of thy strange garb. For truly, thou art a strange sight."

"I am Breunor le Noire and soon you will know that I am of good kin. This coat I wear is token of vow made for vengeance. So, I found it on my slain father and I seek his slayer. This day, oh King, I go forth content, if you make promise that should I perform knightly deed you will dub me knight of yours."

"Go thou forth, then. We doubt not that thou wilt prove thy true valor and be worthy of knighthood. Yet proof must be there."

On this selfsame day, Breunor le Noire departed.

Next morn, the King together with Sir Launcelot, Sir Percival, Sir Gawaine, Sir Pellimore, Sir Gilbert, Sir Neil and Sir Dagonet, indeed a right goodly party, prepared to depart. Nor did they purpose to return until they met with Sir Tristram, for King Arthur was of great desire to have this good knight as one of the Round Table.

Now as these, the flower of King Arthur's court, were waiting for Sir Dagonet who was to be with them and who had delayed, Sir Launcelot saw Allan the boy watching them from the side. Saw too, the great wish in the lad's eyes. Nor did Allan see himself observed for Sir Launcelot was not then with the others.

A thought came to this fine spirited knight and it brought great and smiling good humor to his lips. He rode to Sir Percival's side and the two whispered for many moments. Then did the two speak to the King and he laughed, but did not turn to gaze at the boy. Sir Gawaine now joined in the whis-

pering. Then did all four laugh with great merriment. So Sir Pellimore and the other knights inquired the cause for the merriment and, being told, laughed too. Kindly was the laughter, strong men these who could yet be gentle. Sir Launcelot now turned and rode hard at the boy.

"And wherefore, lad," and dark was his frown and greatly wroth he seemed, "do you stand here watching? Rude staring yours and no fit homage to pay your betters. Perchance, we may all be displeased, the King, Sir Percival, and all of us."

Now the lad's eyes clouded. To have displeased these knights, the greatest men in all the world, for so he thought them. Then and there he wished he could die. Woe had the knight's words brought to him.

"Indeed, and I meant no disrespect, Sir Launcelot. Indeed—" and said no more for he knew he would weep if he spoke further. So he saw not the dancing laughter in the knight's eye, nor the wide grins on the faces of the others.

"Yet we must punish thee, lad. So then prepare you to accompany us. Get your horse at once. Nor will we listen to any prayer you may make for not going because of your youth."

Agape, Allan turned to look at him. For he knew he could not have heard aright. But now, as he looked, he saw that Sir Launcelot was laughing and then as he turned wondering, he saw his own lord and the King and the other knights watching him with great glee.

"You mean then, that I—I—may go with all of you?" And then so that there would be no chance of its being otherwise, he rushed in mad haste to get his horse. Joy was the wings which made his feet fly. He came back in quick time, a bit uncertain, riding forward slowly, diffidently, and stopped a little way from them, awaiting word. Then did Sir Launcelot ride to him and place kindly arm about the youth and bring him among them all.

Now Sir Dagonet was with them and they rode forth. With the equipage came the hounds, for the first day of their journey was to be given over to hunting. There came also the master of the hounds who was to return with them at the close of the hunt.

None other than the great Launcelot rode with Allan and none sat straighter and more at ease in his saddle than the boy as they passed the Queen, the Lady Olande, her two

daughters and many other ladies of the realm. Nor did the boy see any other than the minx Yosalinde. But she—she did not seem to find him among the knights, yet he wondered how she could help but see him. He would have liked to call to her, "See, here am I among all these brave knights." Instead he rode past very erect. If she would not see him, what matter, since, he was there, one of the company.

Then, of a sudden, she smiled straight at him. So that for him was the full glory of the world. And we doubt not, for that smile he would have fought the bravest knight in all the world and found man's strength therein.

Now the company found itself in the woods and many hours journey away. So they rode hard for they liked not to tarry on the road.

Long after midday, King Arthur and his men spread out for the hunt. The forest in which they now found themselves held game and wild animals in plenty. Soon thereafter did the hounds give tongue for they had found the scent. No mean prey had they found though, for the quarry gave them a long race. Close behind the hounds came King Arthur and almost as close, Sir Percival and Sir Launcelot.

[74]

Now, at last, the stag, a noble animal with wondrous horns, lithe body and beautifully shaped limbs was at bay. Straight and true, at its throat, flew the leader of the pack, and sank its teeth deep into it, while above the King blew loud and long the death note of the chase. No need for other hounds nor for weapons of the men.

Dark had stolen over the forest when the men with huge appetites came to sup. Juicy venison·steak was there, so was the wild duck and the pheasant in plenty. To the full they ate as did the few men at arms that were with them.

Yet none stayed awake long thereafter. It had been an arduous day. Allan alone was wide-awake; his eyes would not close. And he knew of a certainty that he was the most fortunate lad in all the world. When he should become a man, he would be—well, he was not certain whether he would be like unto the King, Sir Percival or Sir Launcelot. Yes, he did know, he would be like them all. Now there came mixed thoughts of a maid who waved her hand and smiled at him. And he felt of a precious ring upon his finger.

So now his eyes closed; he found himself seeking the Holy Grail. And during all of the night dreamed that he had found it.

## CHAPTER ELEVEN

# Allan Meets a Stranger

THE noble cortege, after the first day's hunt, continued on its journey.

It had reached Leek, in Stafford on the morn of the fifth day ere word came of Sir Tristram. Here, was heard from some, Sir Tristram was then on way to Scotland, and from still others, that he was bound for Kinkenadon in Wales.

"By my faith," spoke Sir Gawaine," there are none that are more ready to testify to Sir Tristram's greatness and ability, too. Yet still, have I many doubts as to his being both on way to Scotland and to Wales as well."

"If it were left to me," said Sir Dagonet, "I would hie me to Ireland. A likely spot to find him, say I. For there are none who have said that they know of the good knight's journey thitherward."

"We, for ourselves, think it best," the king interrupted, "to tarry here this day. Our comrade, Pellimore, expresses

great desire to have us partake of his hospitality and we are fain, so to do. What say you?"

"It were wisdom to do so, methinks," agreed Sir Percival. "Tomorrow we may find here some further news of Sir Tristram's way."

"Aye, sir knights," added Sir Launcelot, "for we need must know whether we continue our travel north or west from this point."

So all of them were housed within the castle walls. And Sir Pellimcre spread bounteous feast before his guests at midday for he held it high honor to be host to such as these.

Now, as the repast had been completed, Allan grew restless. He was of a mind to ride forth and so craved permission from Sir Percival who gave ready consent.

Forth he went and rode for many an hour. And then, since the day had great heat, he found himself turn drowsy. Thereupon finding a pleasant, shaded spot, he quickly made a couch of cedar boughs and soon was fast asleep.

It seemed to the boy he had slept but few moments when his eyes opened wide with the certainty that other eyes were

directed upon him. Nor was this mere fancy nor dream. Near him sat a monk, and from under the black hood the face that peered forth at him was gaunt, cadavorous, with eyes that seemed to burn straight through the lad. But for the eyes, this figure could well have been carven, so still and immovable did it sit there and gaze at the youth. Nor did the monk speak for many minutes even though he must have known that the boy was awake and watching him.

The sun now hung low in the sky. Allan knew that he must have been asleep for at least two hours. He knew, too, that he should rise and return to the castle, since the hour was already late and his time overspent. Yet did the monk's eyes hold him to the spot. Nor was the thing that held him there fear; rather could it be described as the feeling one has before a devout, sacred and holy presence. Despite the holy man's unworthy aspect he inspired no fear in the lad.

"Allan, boy," and the lad wondered that the monk knew him by name, "two things I know have been chief in your thoughts these days. Kindly was the monk's tone. "What then are these two things?"

No thought had the boy of the oddness of the monk's

words, nor of his questions.  Nor of the fact that the monk
seemed to be there present.  Somehow, the whole of it took
on some great purport.  Allan stopped not to wonder, which
the two things the monk mentioned were uppermost in his mind
but straightway made reply.

"Strange monk, I think and dream of the Holy Grail.
And think too of Yosalinde, sister to my Lord Percival.  And
of nought else so much.  But pray you, holy father, who are
you?

"Truth, lad.  As to who I am or as to where I come,
know you this.  I come to you from that same place as do all
dreams.

"Aye lad.  Dreaming and fancying shall ever be yours.
These son, shall bring you the visions of tomorrow and many
another day.

"I have come to tell you this, lad.  But two years or more
and you shall start in earnest on your search for the Grail.
And whether you find the same, I shall not and cannot say,
for the finding depends on you.  The way shall be hard,
youth of many dreams, though you will have help and guidance,
too.  But the great inspiration for it all shall come to you
from the second of these, your two big thoughts.

[79]

"I sought you many a day, lad. Merlin has sounded the message for me to all the knights of Britain. Once before, years ago, I came to find the likely seeker for the Grail and thought that I had found him. Yet did the crucible's test find some alloy and so I had need to come again.

"Then," said Allan but barely comprehending, "you are none other than Sir Joseph of Armathea."

"Lad, it matters not as to who and what I am. It is of you, we are now concerned. Dear, dear, lad, they shall name you again and the name which shall be yours shall ever after be symbolic with the very best that manhood holds."

"Go your way, now. For I must speak with many more this day ere I return. A knight comes but now, with whom I must hold counsel. And I would fain speak to him, alone."

"True, father, I had best go. For Sir Percival will think me thoughtless, if not worse. As to what you have said, I can do but that best which is in me and ever seek to make that best better. And so, I ask your blessing."

The boy knelt. The monk, lean, black cowled, eyes glowing with a light that held the supernatural, placed hand

upon the boy's head and gave him blessing. So then the boy mounted horse and was away.

He rode hard for he held great anxiety to return quickly. And all the time he rode he thought of the things the strange monk had told him. Some of it, he did not altogether understand. That was because of his youthfulness. It was to come back to him when many months had passed. This however, he knew, he was destined to make search for the Holy Grail. For so, the holy man had ordained.

Sir Percival, a bit anxious, was waiting for the lad when he returned.

"I went far and then fell asleep," Allan explained. "Nor did I awaken until the sun hung low." He did not speak of the meeting with the monk.

"It is well you are back, lad. For I was fast growing worried over the lateness of your return. Turn in then. I wot not, but that food will be found for you on which you can sup. Sir Launcelot went forth some hours ago. I fancy he went in search of you, though he would not admit this to be the purpose of his departure."

## CHAPTER TWELVE

# The Stranger and Sir Launcelot

L ET US then turn to Sir Launcelot now making his way
along the road over which Allan had been seen to depart.
Though the knight had denied that he purposed to seek the lad,
yet had his horse taken that way.   A growing fondness for the
boy which he had not made too obvious, for it was not his wont
to show too easily his feelings.   Display or show of emotion ever
embarrassed him.   He had noted the long absence of Allan
and so had mounted his horse intent to all appearance on a short
canter.

Half way to where Allan had made his couch, the road
over which he had ridden branched right and left and some
miles down came together again.   Now when Allan returned
he took the road to his right having ridden the other way earlier
in the day.   Sir Launcelot made for the road to the right of
him and so missed the boy returning.

He found himself at the place at which the boy had slept.
He dismounted to observe more closely.   Then he beheld the
holy man as he stepped from the shadows.

"Good day to you, holy father," the knight greeted him.

"God's blessing stay with thee, son. I have been expecting thee."

"Nay, father, not me. Other knight, mayhap. For I knew not myself I would be here."

"Yet did I know, Sir Launcelot. You came here to seek the youth Allan and knew not that you came in obedience to greater will than your own. And having come, you must, prithee, listen to the things that must be told you."

"Launcelot," and the monk spoke sternly and yet with great sadness, "as measured by men thou art the bravest knight in Christendom. Chilvalrous, strong, yet gentle and ever ready to succor the weak and distressed. Your name shall be emblazoned as symbolic of chivalry." The strange man paused for a time.

"I speak now of the Holy Grail," he resumed. "Who would be better fitted to seek and find the Holy Grail? Are there any who hold greater desire to find the same? And who seeks to make himself more worthy?"

"And yet, though you seek until Judgment Day you

will never find it.   In the innermost soul of you, you know it to
be so.   The pity of it."

"Strange monk," and a dull red mantled the knight's
cheeks, "those are bold words you speak.   None but Launcelot
himself can tell the things he may or may not do.   And since
I am not in search of father confessor, nor since I sought not
this meeting, I pray thee offer not your counsel nor advice."

"The truth, then, sears, sir knight!"   Now the monk's
eyes flashed.   Straight and tall he stood and his lean figure
held so much of that which was not earthly, that even the
mighty Launcelot was daunted.

"Who then has more right or reason to tell you of
these things.   It is I who first picked you, long since, as likely
finder of the Holy Grail.   And when I found you slipping ever
so little, and well you know wherein you have failed me, I
sent Merlin to all of you.   For since he on whom I had built
my faith could not measure to the test I had strong need to
find someone else.

"For Britain must hold the Grail.   Somewhere in it, there
must be the man who measures up to the test, high though it
be."

"Son, son, the things you could have done. The fineness of you, coarsened by the temptations you have met and not over-come. The joy you have found in things that are sordid and count for so little."

Low hung the knight's head. His anger had left him now. In its stead was a deep humility.

"Father, you bare my soul. And yet have I striven. High did I hold the ideals which first inspired me, I have over-come much, have tried to keep to the high set purpose. Yet I am but common clay, after all."

"Nay, nay son. I would all men held half thy nobility. Only," and now the monk's tone was again kindly, "there are some we weigh on much finer scales than others. We ask more of them, seek more from them. Forgive less, too. Perhaps we are wrong to desire so much from any mortal soul. Yet have we faith,—we believe."

"I find no complaint, holy father, in the measure you have set for me. For I saw the things, I had the vision to see them. Saw too, the things that were wrong even as I did these things."

"Yet, my son, a great task shall be yours. Now of the boy Allan." The monk paused.

"What of him, father? A fine lad is he. So young, yet is he too, to be burdened with great responsibilities? I pray thee, let him keep his youth."

"Launcelot, my son, when will you grow to thy true self? For there lies your failure. You who took your responsibilities as burdens, when you should have found great joy in that they were yours. Yet, now lister to me as to this boy Allan. I have seen him this day, have spoken to him of the Holy Grail. A dreaming youth, yet is he fired by fine inspiration and great ideals. He is ordained to seek it. That holds no strangeness for there are many such. As to whether he finds it or not is dependent upon him, as it was once upon yourself. And since you cannot find it, seek it as you will, I charge you with helping him keep clean souled. Should he do so, ere many years will pass, he may find it. For you, there will be the joy, the glory of service, of having helped. Without your help, success for him will be so much less likely. Will you help him Launcelot? Think well before you make reply."

Not at once did Sir Launcelot answer. Yet it was the best within him that did give final utterance.

"I promise you father, that such help as I can give the lad

I shall. Much have I learned. And with these things that I have learned he shall be guided. No bitterness mine. Since I am not to be the finder of the Holy Grail, I pledge you now my aid to Alian."

"Launcelot, so little fails you for that needed greatness. None have I loved so much. If you have sinned you have been great and glorious even in the sinning.

"Never have you been finer than now. Allan will need your help, your strength. There shall be a maid too, to help him. The threads have also been woven for that now. When the time shall come, you will call this lad Galahad, the Chaste. Treat him ever as your son, Launcelot."

"Son and comrade, too, he shall be for me. Father, I thank you."

"So then I go, son. I could not love you more were you less a mortal sinner."

## CHAPTER THIRTEEN

# The Party Divides

WHEN the morning came there was great indecision as to the further way, for no new information had come of Sir Tristram. Sir Gawaine now spoke for going north to Scotland. So too, was Sir Pellimore minded and Sir Gilbert as well. But Sir Percival spoke for Wales and so did Sir Neil.

"As for me," said Sir Dagonet, "I pick Wales, since Kinkenadon is the nearer to Ireland. My fool's head still fancies that we shall have need to turn there ere we shall find this errant knight."

Neither the King nor Sir Launcelot up to this time had expressed a choice. But now the King vouchsafed a plan.

"It seems to us good plan for our party to divide. Some of us to go north, some west. You Launcelot could well go with one party and we with the other. What say you friends?"

That plan suited them all. So then the King went with Sir Gawaine, Sir Pellimore, and Sir Gilbert, while Sir Launcelot accompanied Sir Percival, Sir Neil, Sir Dagonet and Allan. With each party, too, went three men-at-arms.

Our way shall be with Sir Percival.

At the end of the first half day they found themselves near the crossroads of Nantwich.

"We must soon find place for food," remarked Sir Percival and lustily they all agreed.

"See you castle beyond yonder crossroads?" questioned Sir Neil, "Sir Manstor lives there with his three brothers. Right skilful knights are these but woe the lone stranger who passes by. For these are villainous four."

"Right bitterly do you speak of them, Neil," remarked Sir Launcelot. "And why?"

"I pray fortune to permit me to meet with this Manstor. I stopped there for food one day. Then did this knight, his brothers by his side, demand the bag of gold I carried with me. Nor would single one among them battle with me. It would have fared ill with me but for two knights who passing by, came to my aid."

"Our vow," said Sir Launcelot thoughtfully, "is to find Sir Tristram. Yet can I see no harm in straying from our way an hour or two, can you, Percival?"

"Not if there is promise of such entertainment as this," was the reply.

"These knights," interrupted Sir Neil, "have stomach for neither joust nor other encounter when the odds are not with them. Nor will they venture to impede our way unless we number less than they."

"If greater or equal number withholds them," said Sir Dagonet. "I would favor them and withdraw. Then would there be one less doughty sword."

"Aye, Dagonet, we know your unselfish spirit," said Sir Neil and laughed.

"The knight does not live who has bested me, nevertheless," replied the jester, with pretended heat.

"The knight does not live who has had the chance," said Sir Percival. "Yet we love you none the less, brother."

Said now Sir Launcelot: "One of us could ride ahead. And, perchance, these scheming knights will think that easy prey comes and so strive to impede the way. Then when they bear down upon him we can appear and give them such entertainment as they have not had in many a day."

Now one of the men-at-arms came forward.

"And if you will, masters, yonder cruel knight is cruel master as well. And he holds my own brother within his prison walls for small cause. So I pray you, masters, succor him."

"Of a surety, Wonkin," said Sir Percival, "we shall make every effort to set your brother free. Neil and I shall go forward and so find ourselves seemingly enmeshed by them. Then will you, at proper time, Launcelot, come forward. And if Dagonet so wishes, he can protect our rear."

The two knights then hurried on. They had not far to go to the turn of the road and there the four knights within the castle grounds, seeing them, stood watching for a moment or so. Then each mounted his horse and in armor, rode forth from within the walls.

"We are knights on way to Wales," said Sir Percival in mild tone. "We seek food for our midday meal."

"Food we will give you right gladly," replied the oldest of the four. "But ask in payment such gold as you may have."

"That would be poor bargain," replied Sir Percival, still mild spoken. "We had liefer go our way to place which seeks not such high pay."

"That may you well do, strangers, yet must you still leave your gold behind. For we have great need of it."

"Yet no greater need for it than have we. Come, comrade, we must be on our way." So spoke Sir Percival to Sir Neil. And now the robber knights were certain that these

were but timid men. So out came their swords as they rode at
the two. But they found them ready and watchful. And
though the odds were two to one, it was not hard matter to hold
the robbers off until Sir Launcelot came charging into the
melee.

As the four robbers turned to the newcomer and beheld
his shield and armor, they knew that it was Launcelot. And
knew too that this was trap set for them. Thereupon did Sir
Manstor withdraw for the moment from the struggle and blow
horn he carried—two long and one short note.

One of the brothers had already been unhorsed and most
grievously wounded. Sir Manstor now came back to the aid
of his brothers and of them all he was most skillful. So Sir
Launcelot turned to him and him the robber knight found more
than a match.

But from within the walls came forty and more men at
arms, some with bow and arrow and others with club and mace.
And with them, two other knights.

When Sir Launcelot saw these, he called to his comrades.
"Hard at them, hard."

For he had in mind to down these three before the others
came.

Then did the three, that is, Launcelot, Percival and Neil with wondrous strength of arm, each by mighty blow, bring rider to the ground. And Sir Manstor was dead because of the fearful blow of Sir Launcelot. The other two were asprawl on the ground and but barely moving.

"I call this right skillfully done," said Sir Dagonet who now came toward them. He had watched but had not joined in the struggle.

Now, Wonkin and the two men at arms were there and so was Allan.

"Will you, good men, try out your bows on these hinds who are coming thitherward?" said Sir Percival.

Straightway then there flew three well aimed arrows. Then others flew and now answering arrows from the oncomers. But these did not harm for Wonkin and the other two stood under cover of trees and so were not easy targets.

Twice more they let their arrows fly and five men of the forty had been stopped.

Now as the others came at them with clubs and mace, Sir Launcelot commanded Wonkin and the other two to withdraw a hundred pace and from there continue to let their arrows fly.

And this was great wisdom for else the three could not have long withstood the large number.

So now the knights with their great lances fought off the villains and the two knights who were with them. Very few who came within the reach of the long weapons escaped. And from their place the three men at arms shot arrow after arrow into the attackers.

Three of the knaves had hold of Sir Percival's horse and thereupon others swarmed upon him and what with the blows of their maces and clubs, he was in sorry plight. Nor could Sir Launcelot turn to help him for he was in great conflict with the two knights and a large number of them on foot and Sir Neil equally so. As for Allan he had already ridden down two of the attackers and had brought his weapon which was cross between sword and dagger down upon their skulls. Now as he turned he saw the plight of his lord. So did Sir Dagonet, who though timid had up to then made some ado to help. Whereupon both sped hard to Sir Percival's aid. And so skillful was the boy that he hewed down several of the knaves and Sir Dagonet too, soon found that others of Sir Percival's attackers were turning their attention to him. All of which

gave needed time for Sir Percival to escape from his difficulty, draw sword and begin anew.

Now Sir Launcelot brought down the two knights and the others like wolves stood off snarling at him, yet out of reach. Sir Neil too was freer.

There were but ten of the attackers now. The others were either strewn about the ground or were making their escape. And of these ten, two even then were brought down by the arrows of Wonkin and his two comrades.

Whereupon the last of the attackers turned and made haste to fly, the three archers in close pursuit.

"These hinds would fair have overswarmed me had not the boy and Dagonet come to my aid," remarked Sir Percival as he lifted his helmet from his head.

"How then, Allan, did you like the affray?" inquired Sir Launcelot.

"Greatly," replied the lad. "But I had wish I carried a lance instead of this, which is neither dagger nor sword."

"Right soon, shall these be yours as well, lad. Yet now we have earned such food as we may find within the castle. And I wot not," added Sir Percival, "many prisoners, too, who will be glad of freedom."

## CHAPTER FOURTEEN

# King Mark's Foul Plan

SIR NEIL and Sir Dagonet now loudly summoned the castle servants before them but there were none to answer. So they prepared kitchenward where they found the wretches in great affright not knowing what dire fate was to befall them. Yet they, when assured that naught was intended against them, eagerly hastened to obey the commands of the good knights to prepare a sumptuous meal.

Sir Launcelot, Sir Percival and the other knights made their way to the dungeon. And truly they found a sad sight there. Though a large place, yet was it overly crowded. In one place they found six knights, an unhappy six, three of whom had been imprisoned for many months, two had been made captives within the fortnight and one had joined this joyless group but two days before.

"Aye," one of the first three explained to them," it is through God's mercy that we still live. There were three others with us, two of whom were already here when this dire mis-

fortune befell us and one who came some weeks later. These three could not survive the foulness of this hole."

But now Sir Percival was seen to speak to the lone knight, the one who had been made prisoner last of all. A melancholy figure, he did not seem to realize that release had come with the advent of these knights. In fact, through all the hubbub he seemed to have been lost within himself. No doubt, they were bitter thoughts that possessed him and at such times one is verily unmindful of things about him. Nor did this knight seem mindful of the words spoken by Sir Percival for he made no answer and lost none of his brooding air.

Yet, of a sudden, he seemed to awaken. For Sir Percival who had not been able to place him at first, had at last realized who the stranger was.

"Who are you?" the other questioned in turn rubbing his eyes. "And these other knights? But then, I know you all. How came you here, Sir Percival?"

When he was told, some of his dejection left him.

"Mine was truly a great unhappiness. These four robber knights did beset me. And when I was overcome they demanded great ransom which I had no means wherewith to satisfy. Then, when I heard the tale of how long these fellow prisoners had been here I was greatly discouraged as to carrying out my intent to prove to King Arthur my worthiness for knighthood."

In the meanwhile, Sir Launcelot and Allan had made their way to where the imprisoned yeomen and hinds had been kept. Here there were more than fifty and a sad sight they were. It brought a great gulp of pity into Allan's throat and unbidden tears came to his eyes. Sir Launcelot too was moved. Some of the prisoners were so weak they could hardly move. Wonkin had found his brother almost at once and theirs was a happy meeting.

"Go you up, good Allan, and order that food be brought for these wretches. And see to it that there is plenty of it."

Allan gladly went and repeated Sir Launcelot's orders which the servants made great haste to obey.

So that all within the castle, fared well that day. And when Sir Launcelot and his party were ready to continue their journey the next morning, there was with them Breunor le

Noire and an added number of yeomen picked from the men who had been prisoners.

Just before departure, Sir Percival went to the two brothers of Sir Manstor who still were living, the other had not lived an hour.

"Sir Knights, we leave you now. Take you heed from this day's happenings that such outlawry as yours brings just punishment. Remember, too, that King Arthur and all his knights will be ever watchful that you conduct yourself in knightly ways. Woe betide you, if you do not."

The knights made no reply. Grievously wounded, with their brothers dead, they were in no mood for words. Yet must the truth of Sir Percival's words have been in their minds.

Onward now went Sir Launcelot's party. Through that and the next day they made their way and were well in Cornwall without further untoward happening. Everywhere, the party made inquiries as to the whereabouts of Sir Tristram and from such news as they were able to gather they felt assured that they had taken the right way and that King Arthur and the men with him were on a false trail.

[99]

It was on this day that they met with two knights who made them friendly greetings and finding out the purpose of their journey pretended not to know the whereabouts of Sir Tristram. Nor would they stay for any length of time giving as reason therefore great need of urgency on their part. Yet when these two knights had but gone a little way they turned, in great haste along another road. The end of the day found them in the presence of King Mark of Cornwall who had no great love for King Arthur nor for any of his knights and who would do any or all of them great harm could he do so without discovery.

"Who then is this party?" inquired the King after listening.

"They number but few," replied one of the knights. "Sir Launcelot, Sir Percival, Sir Neil, and one other, and that fool who is jester to Arthur. A boy is there too and fifteen men-at-arms."

"You speak truly," replied the king, "as to their being few in number but I would that two of these few, were not Launcelot and Percival. Yet even with these two we should be able to overcome them. And in that way I shall find some

recompense for the many slights and haughty overbearingness of Arthur and his men." As he so spoke, King Mark's face plainly showed its cruelty and craft.

"Will you, good Bruyan, call Sir Bertram and Sir Pendore to me? And be sure to return for we must be speedy should we decide that it is wise for us to take any step for their discomforture."

Now as Bruyan returned with the two aforementioned, there also came into the room a yeoman who served Sir Pendore. But of him neither the king nor any of the knights took notice but instead immediately began discussion as to the wisdom of waylaying these knights of King Arthur who were now in Cornwall.

Whether King Mark knew this to be so or not, yet of all his court, there were no two who had more reason to hate Sir Launcelot than Sir Bertram and Sir Pendore. For Sir Launcelot had come upon them once when they were in the midst of tormenting two holy men having first taken from them a paltry purse which these two monks were carrying for worthy purpose. Then when Sir Launcelot had asked that they desist and return the holy men's purse they had replied with foul

tongue and had made for him. Soon, however, they found that this single knight was master of them both and would they then have complied with his requests. However, Sir Launcelot who was ever slow to anger was now in great rage and he had taken them to the castle grounds of Sir Gawaine and there, before a large number he told of what had happened. And while fair ladies laughed at them and while men looked at them as they would at hinds, Sir Launcelot had taken the flat of his sword and had brought it down on both. Then he had asked two yeomen to club them from the castle grounds since they were unfit to be in the company of knights. This the yeomen had done right lustily.

Neither Sir Pendore nor Sir Bertram had ever made mention of this event. But there was no one in all of Britain whom they so fully hated as Sir Launcelot. Now, there seemed likely chance for revenge.

"How many men can you muster?" asked Sir Bertram, speaking not over anxiously yet with meaning looked at Sir Pendore.

"Seven score or more" replied the king of Cornwall.

"I would have more," replied Sir Pendore. "What with Percival and Launcelot and this Neil whom I know not, one must make it more than certain."

It was at this point that the yeoman who was busily at work over the weapons, cleaning them and putting them into perfect condition, as none other in Cornwall could do, had become interested. Sir Percival?

It was this Sir Percival, knight of the Round Table, who had saved the father of this yeoman from the deadly mace of one of his men in one of many melees. It was but a small thing to the knight, long forgotten no doubt, but to Walker, the son of the man who was saved, it meant that he was in debt to this knight. So now he listened, interested. Then too, he had no great love for his master who was never kindly and he had decided long ago that he would find a new master when the opportunity offered.

"I shall find more men, if I can," Mark offered in reply to Sir Pendore's suggestion. Nor did it seem strange to him that the knight should think that odds of seven to one were not enough.

"Where are these knights?" asked Sir Bertram.

Sir Bruyan told him, the yeoman listening all the while.

"Let us then be off within thrice this hour," Mark conclud-
ed. "Get you as many men ready as you can," he said to Sir
Bertram and to Sir Pendore who were his chiefs.

Walker, the yeoman, soon had completed his work. Thereupon he made his way into the forest to find him, who was best
friend of his, to get advice as to what to do.

He, whom he sought, was none other than our old friend
Gouvernail, who, of course, was not far from Sir Tristram,
his master.

Though he had long since severed fealty to King Mark,
Sir Tristram had returned near unto the court because of the
love he bore one of the damsels who was in it. It was Walker
who had carried the messages Gouvernail had brought from his
master to this same lady.

Walker soon came to the hiding place of his friend.

"What ho?" asked Gouvernail. "What brings you here
at this unseemly hour?"

"I need your advice," replied Walker. My poor head
carries too great a muddle."

"You come to one who can offer but poor solace there," replied Gouvernail. "If it were trusty arm, good club or something belike, you could well come to me. But speak, what troubles you?"

So Walker told him. Except that at first he made no mention of names.

"Keep you from it," advised Gouvernail. "It is the business of your betters and not of your meddling."

"Yet had Sir Percival done this thing for my father, and if he would, he could have thought the same,—that it was not his affair but an affair of hind or yeoman."

"Is this Percival, he who is of King Arthur's court?" asked Gouvernail.

"Aye," replied Walker, nodding his head. "Do you know him?"

"Somewhat. Who else is there?" he further questioned, now interested.

"Sir Launcelot, Sir Neil and some others."

"Did they speak of a boy being there?"

"I do not remember.   Yet I seem to recall that they did," replied Walker.

"I will help you.   Come," and Gouvernail took his friend but a little way to where Sir Tristram was lodging.

Sir Tristram seated himself and listened to the two.   He understood at once.

"When did King Mark say that he would start with his men?" he asked Walker.

"In three hours, Sir Knight," the man answered.

"Good.   Let us be off.   Good Gouvernail, get you my mail ready for I would don it."

Within the half hour Sir Tristram with the two yeomen were on their way to meet Sir Percival and Sir Launcelot.   So, strangely, they who sought him, were to find him come among them.

## CHAPTER FIFTEEN

# The Weasel's Nest

"GREETING, good knights," he announced. "I am Sir Tristram."

Nothing could have thrown Sir Launcelot's party into greater astonishment. And yet no news could have been pleasanter.

"Right glad are we to see you, Sir Tristram, since we have sought you for a great number of days. I am Sir Launcelot. Here is Sir Percival." And so this knight announced them all.

The two knights, Sir Tristram on the one hand, Sir Launcelot, on the other, observed each other. Each of them found much to like in the other. Then and there was the beginning of a friendship that was to last until the day of Sir Tristram's death.

After the first few moments, had passed, Sir Tristram came to the reason for his coming among them.

That the danger was grave, they knew at once. King Mark was cruel and crafty. He would not venture this attempt unless he were certain that he had great numbers behind him.

"My thought seems to be to retire to the nearest castle and there defend ourselves as best we can," said Sir Percival.

"A right kindly thing, this of yours, Sir Tristram, to bring us this news. And if we come out of this, I hope that I shall be able to find you at any place you bespeak," Sir Launcelot remarked.

"The kindness is on the part of this man here." And Sir Tristram told them of Walker. "Need I say that I stay with you and share in your fortune such as it is. It should offer great sport and I would not miss it, if I could."

Sir Launcelot nodded his head nor did he make any further demur.

"And you two?" he now asked of Gouvernail and Walker.

"Oh, I," replied Sir Gouvernail, "I find my place where my master is."

"And I?" added Walker. "I owe something to Sir Percival and so I too will stay."

"Well then, perhaps we may keep them off, though not so easily," said Sir Neil.

"We can but try," added Sir Launcelot.

But now Sir Dagonet, jester and fool, made his way forward.

"Spoke you of finding castle?" he asked of Sir Percival.

Sir Percival nodded his head.

"Good man," Sir Dagonet spoke now to Walker. "Did this weasel king say aught as to the number of men he would send against us?"

"Only, master, that when he mentioned that he would send one hundred or more and with them twenty knights, one there, thought that number not enough and advised that the king add to it. Which the king said he would do."

"The more the better," said Sir Dagonet.

"A strange wish," said Sir Neil. "But then you are fool and that wish belongs to a fool."

"Yet not such a great fool after all," spoke up Sir Launcelot. "Truly Dagonet, I often wonder at you. For here is what is in Dagonet's mind. Since the weasel comes after us and leaves his home empty, why not go to the home of the weasel?"

Such a laugh now went up. For all of these knights saw that this would be a deed that would ring throughout Britain and if successful, make Mark the laughing stock of the land.

But after the laughter, Sir Tristram spoke, "I ask a strange thing, good knights, and hope it will receive favor in your eyes. King Mark has been a strange uncle to me. He has treated me scurvily oft enough. Yet when, if we come through this event as we hope, I would that you hold no further ill will against him. Understand me well. I ask for naught, if any among us are hurt at his hand, for then he deserves all that comes to him. But if we come through so that all can laugh at him, then I ask you to forget the ill will for which he gives you such good cause. For after all, he is blood kin of mine, a sorry thing, yet which I cannot forget." And now the knight waited answer.

Now all the knights turned to Sir Tristram and there was something about him that made them nod their heads in assent.

"Then do we promise this thing, you ask," said Percival. "So now let us go to the weasel's nest."

In great humor and with many jests the men made their way to the road upon which the two knights of King Mark had made their return. And so we find that as the crafty king was making his way forward to the attack, believing that it would be an overpowering surprise, and already counting the fruits of victory, his intended victims were slipping through his clutches and making their way into the last of all places he could imagine.

Now on their way, Sir Percival called the two yeomen, Gouvernail and Walker to him. And though he did not remember the event that Walker narrated yet was he glad he had followed a kindly thought. And Allan too, realized that bread cast upon the water often returns.

"Need you a good yeoman?" ventured Walker hopefully.

"If you are half as good as your friend here, then indeed have I need for you," was Sir Percival's reply.

"I count him my better, Sir Knight," replied Gouvernail.

[111]

"This fool would overpraise me and lead you to expect overmuch," said Walker. I will do my best if you will but try me."

"That I shall," replied the knight. And thereupon the two, Gouvernail and Walker, fell back a little way and came to Allan who was glad of a chance to talk to Gouvernail. And as they rode forward the boy listened to some of the tales and some of the doings of Sir Tristram."

Now in the front there rode, the two, Sir Tristram and Sir Launcelot and with them Sir Dagonet.

"Truly, I often wonder, good Dagonet, wherefore they call you a fool," spoke Sir Launcelot. "Here comes this thought of yours that could come only from the wisest man or the greatest fool. Often, I wonder which you are."

"Yet good Launcelot, since I am I, I know which of these I am. What sooth, what matters it, which you and all of these," and Sir Dagonet pointed to the others with them, "which you think me? If it pleases all of you, it pleases me to be a fool. Howsoever, it is ill wind that does not blow some good and here we have Sir Tristram who is not in Ireland though I had reason for believing him there."

"Faith, friend, and I had but decided that I would journey henceward within two days," replied Sir Tristram wonderingly.

"See you then, Launcelot. I made but a fool's guess. Had I been a wise man I would not have been two days ahead of Sir Tristram."

Now Sir Tristram who knew the way advised silence. For they were nearing the great castle walls. When they came thereto they found the gates closed and the drawbridge up.

Then did Sir Tristram make call to those within. And these mistaking this for the party tha' had gone therefrom hastened to obey and lowered the drawbridge and unlocked the gates. And then found themselves facing strange knights, a strange party. And of all of them they only recognized Sir Tristram.

Then would they have made great ado to close the gates but it was too late.

"Tell you all within these gates, that we shall treat none harshly except those who would make trouble."

So when Sir Percival's party was safely esconced, Sir Tristram left them for a few moments. A few moments that lasted

into the half hour. For he went to see his lady love who was even then with the queen.

Nor did the queen treat him as harshly as she might have. Perhaps this was because she felt that they were safe as long as this nephew was with these intruders. Or perhaps she had not favored the ill treatment by her royal spouse of so brave a knight.

And if King Mark and his men had been surprised to find the bird flown, imagine then what must have been their thoughts when they returned and found that they could not enter their own gates. That the bird was there and was shouting defiance at them. And worse yet, that in these shouts of defiance there was laughter and taunt and jest at their expense.

"What now?" asked the cruel and crafty king.

Nor could one of his men tell him.

## CHAPTER SIXTEEN

# To The Rescue

"METHINKS," said King Arthur on the fourth day of their journey into Scotland that we will not find this Sir Tristram. What say you Gawaine?"

"Only that I cannot find it in me to do aught but agree with you," the latter made reply. "And I advise that we return, for had Tristram made his journey hitherward we should long ago have had inkling of it."

"So then, we return today, friends," Arthur announced to his knights. "We have it in us to hope that Percival and Launcelot have had better fortune than we."

And none loath, the party joyously made preparations for return. It had been an eventless search for the brave knight, Tristram, and these men hated inactivity.

"What say you, to sending someone of us to Cadoris announcing that we shall pay him a visit of not more than a day?" So queried the king.

"If there is promise of joust and adventure there," said

Pellimore. "I for one can see no harm therein. What matters a day more or less?"

The other knights agreed with Pellimore and as Gawaine pointed out, it was not more than but few leagues from their returnward way.

So the party having first sent Sir Gilbert before them to herald their approach arrived at the court of Cadoris, king of Scotland. And never was king or knights more royally received than was Arthur and his men. Of a truth, there was warm affection for Arthur, and Cadoris and his knights, though they held great rivalry, for the Knights of the Round Table had ever proven honest and worthy opponents.

The stay of the day stretched into the fourth day and not one of King Arthur's party had thought of returning. Jousts were there, much hunting and activity, enough to suit the most exacting. Howsoever, Arthur announced on the fifth day that they could stay but another day.

"Of a truth, am I downright sorry that you must depart. For highly have I been honored by your visit, and as greatly have I enjoyed it." Warm spoken was Cadoris.

"And we shall remember your hospitality for many a day," replied Arthur. "If we but make you half as much at home when you visit us, good Cadoris, we shall feel that we have accomplished much. Is it not so, friends?"

"Truly," assented King Arthur's knights. "And I would, your Majesty, that you make that visit right soon," added Gawaine.

"That we surely will," replied Cadoris heartily.

So King Arthur and his men made their preparations having been much cheered by their stay. And they had turned to their last meal which was a sumptuous one and were greatly enjoying it when a servant of King Cadoris came into the great dining hall and whispered into the ear of Sir Donald, one of the bravest knights in the kingdom of Scotland. He in turn, whispered the news to the king.

"There are two riders without, Arthur, who want word with you," the Scottish King announced. "Shall I ask them to wait until we finish this meal? It were pity to disturb you now and I doubt not their message may wait."

"That may well be so, good friend. Yet, if it disturbs you

not, I shall ask Gawaine here to see these men and find out what message they bear."

Cadoris nodded his head in assent and Gawaine thereupon hastened outside the dining hall.

It was none other than Allan he saw. Allan with Breunor le Noire. Great was his surprise at seeing them and greater still, at their account of what had occurred. And when he heard how Launcelot and Percival and the others, together with Sir Tristram were holding the very castle of King Mark, he shook with a great laughter. So loud was this that the kings and the knights at the dining table heard it and wondering greatly, hurried out to find the cause for it. Forgot their food for the time being in their curiosity.

The king of Britain was no less surprised to see Allan and this stranger whom he but faintly recalled. And to him, to Cadoris, and the assembled knights, the two had to recount again what had occurred. And when the full gist of it came home, Arthur brought down a heavy hand on the shoulder of Cadoris who was shaking with laughter and himself fell into a seat nearby for very faintness at his own mirth. While about him there was great boisterousness and loud guffaws. A

yeoman who had listened eagerly to the account hurried without and himself recounted to the men there what had happened at the court of King Mark. So that there were great shouts, much merriment.

"To think," said King Arthur, "a bare few took King Mark's own castle." I marvel at their impudence and yet it is but what could be expected from such as they."

"As for me," said Gawaine, "I would give all I have to have been there. And all I ever expect to have, to have been near Mark when he realized what had happened."

"Yet," said Arthur now grown serious, "let us hear what Allan and this other brave youth are here for. They did not come this great distance to tell us of their impudence. That, I'll swear."

"Nay, sire," said Allan, who was spokesman because of greater acquaintance with those assembled. "Sir Percival and Sir Launcelot sent Breunor le Noire to you and me with him for aid. For King Mark, furious at the sorry figure he makes has sworn vengeance and has laid siege to those within his castle. Sir Launcelot sent us with this message. That while

they could perhaps make their escape yet they thought that you would wish to come to their aid so that they need not run from King Mark. For they wish to see that king, to look at him. Half the jest they have played lies in that."

"That we will do, of course," replied Arthur. "And though we must first return home to gather our men, yet we will do so quickly and hurry just as quickly to the court of Cornwall. For we too, would like to see Mark, and though we envy your party its good fortune, yet can we share in the jest. Say you not so, friends?

"Aye, sire, that we do. Yet haste is indeed necessary." So spoke both Pellimore and Gawaine.

"Methinks, it would be a right friendly act on your part, Arthur, should you allow me and my men to accompany you. So then there will be no need for you to first return home and thereby save time. For I too," added Cadoris, "would like to call on Mark at this time."

"Come then," said King Arthur. "It would not be in us to refuse you. Let us return to finish our food and both of you, we doubt not must be right hungry by now."

So all of them returned to the dining hall. And Gawaine found room next to him for Allan and Breunor le Noire.

"How long Allan, is it since you left them?" he asked.

"This is our third day," was the boy's reply.

"How did you escape the besiegers?" Arthur, who with the rest was listening now inquired.

"It was done at night, sire. We two climbed over the wall. Two yeomen helped us over. One of King Mark's men saw us and at first mistook us for men from his own camp. Him, Breunor le Noire, gave little time for outcry. We gagged and bound him and then Walker and Gouvernail climbed back for a long rope and lifted him over on the castle side. For we had no wish to have King Mark's men find him and suspect that some of those within had gone for aid."

Now the meal was over. Within another hour King Cadoris had gathered five hundred of his men. King Mark and his men would never have stomach for affray. When the afternoon's sun was in the low western sky, the rescuing party was well on its way.

## CHAPTER SEVENTEEN

# In King Mark's Castle

SO WE return to the doughty few who are behind the walls of the great castle.

"We shall wear out these impudent knaves," King Mark had said after the first great surprise. "Surely they cannot expect to hold out for any great length of time."

"Aye," had agreed the ever present Pendore and Bertram. "And when they are overcome," Sir Pendore had added darkly, "then shall we find our day has come. For Launcelot shall surely suffer."

But the days went and the besiegers found a far greater and more stubborn resistance than they had expected. Their losses were many, due to the skillful archery of the few within. King Mark's castle was of the kind that could only be assailed at two points which was in itself great help to the besieged.

If, perchance, the men of King Mark had had greater stomach for the attack, things might have gone ill with those within. But there were many of the men of this king who favored but

little the quarrel with the besieged, counting it, in their own hearts, a scurvy action on the part of Cornwall's king. And men fight poorly who have such thoughts.

Not that all was well with those within. On this, the eighth day of their occupancy of the castle, the men were a haggard lot. Little sleep had they. Some of them had been wounded, wonder it was that these were so few and that none were dead. Sir Neil was lost to them for the time, Wonkin, too had fought heroically but had fallen, sorely wounded in an attack. Three others had been hurt, and for every man who fell, there grew the greater burden on those who were left. Constant watch, constant need for being present to repel the attackers had left the mark of weariness on Sir Launcelot, Sir Tristram and Sir Percival. Yet these three were a host in themselves as they, with Gouvernail and Walker, set an inspiring example to the rest.

"Faith," said Sir Percival at this moment, "I cannot say that I would not welcome the arrival of Arthur and our men."

"I had never thought sleep so great a luxury," rejoined Sir Tristram.

"Nor I," added Sir Launcelot. "However, do you both

take such little of that now as those knaves who are on the outside permit."

But this neither of the two had in mind to do. Yet Sir Launcelot insisted and only had his way when he promised that he would also take time for sleep after them.

They had, so it seemed to them, but barely fallen asleep, when there was great outcry from both within and without the gates. The men of King Mark had evidently decided on a determined attack with full intention to overcome the stubborn few. In a great mass they came and though many fell and every arrow told yet were they not to be denied. And as they came close to the walls King Mark's men opened wide their ranks and a score of men were seen carrying a bridge to throw over in place of the drawbridge which they could not reach.

"Now has it grown right serious," said Sir Launcelot. "Will you Percival hold these walls while Tristram, I, Gouvernail and Walker, make every effort to see that the bridge does not stay."

There was no time for further words. The four quickly made for the gates. They opened and closed them quickly.

Each held a stave that seemed not unlike a young tree, of which a number were inside the gates.

"Let them place the bridge first," said Sir Launcelot.

Upon them a hail of arrows fell but none were hurt. Gouvernail and Walker were protected for the time in both coats and helmets of steel which Sir Tristram had made them wear.

Now the men of King Mark had thrown the bridge over the embankment. But as the first of them rushed upon it the thick staves of the four men did their work well. Mighty work it was but it was question whether there were four men in all of England who had greater strength than these. And so as the men came rushing over, the bridge seemed moving with them.

A great outcry came from them. The new made bridge, moving slowly at first, now cleared its support, and fell into the depths below carrying twenty men with it. Some managed to get back to safety, some, almost as unfortunate as those who had fallen with the bridge, made their way to the castleside. These Sir Tristram and Sir Launcelot and the two yeomen easily overcame.

From the walls a hail of arrows, stones and javelins were sent on the attackers. The four outside the walls, their work accomplished, returned within. But King Mark and his two lieutenants, of whom one had been on the bridge, were now not the less determined to carry the walls.

The besiegers at the furthermost points were seen to clamber over the walls. They were battering at the gates at which Sir Tristram, Sir Launcelot and a number of the men had taken their stand.

Things indeed looked dark for those within. Sir Percival, for one, had been grievously wounded in the last affray.

But the gates made to withstand against attack held well.

Yet it was now a mere question of time. This, both those within and without fully realized.

"Unless our two messengers find King Arthur," said Sir Tristram calmly and unhurriedly, "it matters but little whether we fight our way out now or later. Is it not so?"

"I have faith in the coming of the king," said Sir Launcelot. "For the boy Allan, I know to be tireless in the performance of such duty. And if I mistake not the other will try his utmost too, for he seeks to be dubbed a knight by our king.

So now down at the gates, now on the walls, sending death and destruction upon the attackers the two knights held their own, fighting hopefully, unyieldingly, hour after hour.

There was a cry of joy now, of exultation from Gouvernail. For his eagle eye espied in the distance a horse and rider, then other horses and other riders.

The faint notes of the slughorn came to their ears. The men on the outside ceased their attack for the moment watching wonderingly, not guessing as yet what all this meant.

From his bed of pain, not far off, Sir Percival called to the two knights.

"Is it Arthur who comes?"

"Methinks so. Yet it seems I see the banners of Scotland. Whether it is men of Cadoris or of Arthur, of what matter?"

"Aye, Launcelot, Scotland is there. But yonder figure is Arthur." So spoke Tristram.

"There too, is Gawaine and Pellimore. And there the boy, Allan. See you him?"

Sir Tristram nodded assent.

Now Mark and his men gathered close together. The king and Sir Pendore and Sir Bertram were in close converse.

Up to the walls came the rescuing party. King Arthur in front frowning, mighty, a majestic figure who seemed to breathe fire and fury.

"What does this mean, Mark? What scurvy trick have you now tried?"

"I found these men within holding my own castle when I returned from a short journey. What else could I do but try to oust them?"

"I know better. If any harm, if but one of my knights is hurt, I shall make you pay right fully."

Now the gates opened wide. There stood Sir Launcelot, and Sir Tristram, both supporting Sir Percival. Into the castle rode King Arthur and King Cadoris.

"Have you been hurt? Who else is wounded? Are any dead?" These were the questions of the king.

So Sir Launcelot told him. And now when the king found that none were dead and he realized how many men Mark

had lost, good humor again came to him. His eyes twinkled merrily.

"Shall we hang this scurvy king?" he asked.

"If you will, sire," said Sir Tristram. "I fancy he has suffered much by now. And since he is uncle of mine I beg of you treat him more gently than he deserves. Let us rather laugh at him. True, there are some of us who have been wounded, but none fatally."

"And after all." said Sir Percival, "see how *much* we can laugh?"

Sir Launcelot too nodded in agreement.

"In truth," King Arthur agreed, "I have found no fancy to act as hangman to him. For knave and villain though he is, yet is he still a king. What say you Cadoris?"

"It is no brew of mine, good Arthur. Yet were I he and you had such good cause to laugh at me, I wonder if I would not rather hang."

So King Arthur turned to King Mark. Laughter was in his eye, mocking laughter. About him the others gathered and these, too, seemed laughing at him.

"I offer you advice, Mark, which so it seems to me, you would do well to heed. Keep not your doors so wide open hereafter. Knaves like these are too apt to accept such hospitality. And, good Mark, when next you go a hunting, I fancy, you had best hunt at home. It is safer and for one thing you are sure to have it. 'Tis a sad state for you to find these men making themselves at home while you are away on so peaceful a mission. 'Tis a sad pity and should not be permitted."

"Tis sad, 'tis sad," said the men about King Arthur.

King Mark scowled in fury. And somehow, it seemed, he scowled most at his own nephew, Tristram.

## CHAPTER EIGHTEEN

# The Kitchen Boy Again

NOW KING Arthur, his knights and all of his men were home once again. Here they found great good humor at their account of the adventure at the castle of King Mark.

Tristram came with them. For many years thereafter he served under King Arthur. Honor and glory he brought to the court of the King and Arthur held him in high esteem as well he might. Between Launcelot and Tristram there grew a great friendship. Each of them believed the other to be the greatest knight in Christendom.

And Allan, too. Now he was a year older. The urge to go forth, strong within him, had grown that day a year earlier, when the strange monk had met him in the forest and told him the things he might do. Youth though he still was, not yet sixteen, he had learnt much. Sir Launcelot and Sir Tristram, too, had spent much time with him—could there have been better teachers? Gouvernail and Walker, as well, taught him

to make the best use of such strength as he had. So that by now he was the equal of many knights, better, too, though none of his teachers would let him know that, and he, secure in his own modesty, unknowing of his great prowess.

The year, too, had brought Sir Kay's kitchen boy once again before the King. Him, Allan had learned to know. Although his friend had never admitted that he was better than his position warranted, Allan was certain of it. When Pentecost had come again he was curious as to what other boons were to be asked of the king by this kitchen boy.

But the day found him away—sent to the castle of Sir Percival, which was a half day's journey. Yet was he not altogether disappointed, for at that castle was Yosalinde, Sir Sir Percival's sister.

Again there were many who sought the favor of the King on this day. There, too, were many knights present and among these were Sir Gawaine, Sir Percival and Sir Launcelot, the three who had been there the year before.

"And so, sire," the kitchen boy said, when the king turned to him, "I have done my work as best I could. Now I crave my two boons."

"These shall be yours, if we have it in us to grant you them. What are these boons you ask?"

"That I be made a knight by Sir Launcelot. Him and him only do I wish to dub me with knighthood. And that furthermore you permit me to take up the first adventure which may need knight to carry same."

"So shall it be. We pray you, however, that you give your name."

"That will I do, sire, after Sir Launcelot had jousted with me, if he then finds me worthy of knighthood."

"Of a sooth," said Sir Kay, "you ask not much. That so brave a knight should joust with a kitchen boy is fit cause for merriment." Loud was that knight's laughter but none joined with him.

"Mayhap," said the strange youth, "it will be your pleasure to joust first with me."

Uncertain seemed Sir Kay for a few moments.

"I promise you, Sir Kay, mine is gentle blood, and you may well combat with me," the kitchen boy added mildly.

Then did the two straightway prepare, horse and armor having been obtained for the younger man.

Not long did they battle however, for the kitchen boy proved Sir Kay's master right quickly. Whereupon, Sir Kay becoming furious, made great ado to wound his opponent. But could not do so; instead, the other brought him down with fearful stroke which crushed through helmet and all.

"If you please, now, Sir Launcelot, to joust with me, I shall find it great honor." So spoke the youth to the knight.

Then there was such a battle as none had seen in many months. Neither of these two brought to play his full strength, yet right cleverly, each struck, counterstruck and brought his skill to play. Much marveled the knight at the youth.

Then finally, Sir Launcelot said.

"Your quarrel and mine, youth, is not so sore, we may not leave off."

"Truly, that is truth," replied the lad. "But it does me good to feel your might."

"So tell me your name, that I may dub you knight. Right gladly will I do so."

"My name," said the other, "is Gareth. I am brother to Gawaine. I made vow to prove myself worthy of knighthood by finding myself able to undergo the mean tasks as well as the noble ones."

So Sir Gawaine came forward wonderingly, to see this brother whom he had not seen since he was a babe.

He made him fond embrace. "Right proud of you am I brother. Proud too, that it is Launcelot, whose knight you shall be."

Then Sir Gareth became knight. And as they made their way again into the great hall, the King beckoned to Sir Gareth.

"Are you still of a mind to take on yourself the first adventure that cometh. For here is one that promises a lengthy time in its fulfillment."

Before the new knight could make answer, Sir Gawaine spoke.

"This sire, is Gareth, my youngest brother. Worthy of knighthood has he proven so far as strength and skill go."

"Then are we right proud to have you among us, nephew. And we pray that you will add lustre to your honored name and to the Round Table as well."

"That, I warrant, he will," vouchsafed Sir Launcelot. "Perchance, it seemeth a wise thing to have Sir Kay feed all our knights in prospect the same fat broth he has furnished Gareth."

"As to the adventure," the King returned. "There came but a little while ago a maiden, Linet, by name, who craves that we send a knight to succor her sister, the fair Dame Lyoness who is besieged in her castle by the Knight of the Red Lawns."

"Good herald," the King continued, "bring you the lady Linet before us."

Into the great hall came a maiden fair. To her the king addressed himself.

"My Lady Linet, and it please you, pray tell us of what manner of siege this knight holds against your sister. If to you it seems of avail, we shall be glad to send a goodly number of our knights and yeomen, too, to raise this siege."

"Nay sire, that I deem not necessary. Only, since I have heard that the knights of the Round Table are the bravest and

"MY LADY, I AM YOUR LOYAL KNIGHT"

best in all Britain, I have come to you that you send one of these
to battle with the Knight of the Red Lawns. A stout knight
is he, many have come to rescue the fair lady who is my sister
but the way is perilous and he hath seven men's strength. So
that I pray you to send the best and bravest knight who is here."

"We would gladly heed your request, good lady. Nor do
we care what manner of knight this is, if Sir Launcelot or Sir
Tristram or any one of ten or twelve more were to go to your
fair sister's rescue. But we have made promise that the next
adventure, which this is, was to be taken up by Sir Gareth
and unless he forego this, there is naught else left for us to do.
What say you, Gareth?"

"I beg you, sire, that you permit me to carry out this adventure. I shall do my utmost to bring it to successful conclusion." So did Gareth reply.

"And I for one, sire, doubt not, that if the adventure can be
carried out successfully, he will do so. For he is as brave and
stout a knight as is among us," added Sir Launcelot.

"Yet is he so young," said the maiden as she sighed. "I
doubt that any of you know how powerful is the knight he
must oppose."

[137]

"Yet will he go," Arthur now decided. "Make you your plans Gareth. The way seems long and I doubt not, you will be disposed to continue on adventure's course, if this should be carried to successful conclusion."

Now the maiden left the great hall. Sir Gareth joined Sir Launcelot, Sir Percival and his brother. As he did so, there came to him, Breunor le Noire.

"I pray you to favor me, good Sir Gareth by permitting me to go with you and gather for myself such adventure as I may."

Sir Gareth pondered for a moment, then made reply.

"I had a mind to ask a boon of Sir Percival yet I can see no reason why it would interfere with your going."

"It is this, Sir Percival. I know how much your page Allan craves for some adventurous journey before he also becomes knight. Be so kind, therefore, and permit him to go with me."

"Truly, it will be Youth seeking adventure. For each of you is indeed youthful." So spoke Sir Gawaine, while Sir Percival thought before making reply.

"What say you, Launcelot?" he finally asked.

"It cannot harm the lad to go with others than ourselves for then he will receive opportunity to test himself. I would say that you permit him, if he wishes it."

"Then may he go," said Sir Percival. "Except that I would wish that one of my yeomen, whose name is Walker, go with you. You will find him useful and a willing knave."

"For that I thank you," replied Gareth. "Tomorrow, my friend," and he turned to Breunor, "we begin our journey."

"I shall be ready," replied Bruenor le Noire.

## CHAPTER NINETEEN

# On Adventure's Way

NOW, as the knights separated, Sir Launcelot, who had donned but part of his armor, called Sir Gareth.

"I would a word with you, Gareth. I pray you to spare me the time."

"Right gladly," said Gareth and seated himself beside the other. Sir Percival, who had a mind to return to them, on seeing them so seated, swerved his horse and passed by them. Nor did they see him.

"See you this sword and shield. Take you these and use them well. They are good weapons and you will find them answering well to urge and parry.

"Yet it is something of far more urge than this that I would speak to you about. I am right glad that you are to have Allan with you. I hope he will find much adventure and many experiences. Listen well to this."

Then did Sir Launcelot tell of the message that had been given both to him and the boy. Told also of the need for Allan to stay the fine and devout lad he was.

"You can help, too. I made promise to Sir Joseph of Armathea that I would do what I can. Since you are knight dubbed by me, I pray you to help me."

" That shall I do right gladly, for I like the youth and his kindly ways. I give you my promise to give him by such example as I may set and in other ways the meaning of knighthood worthy of the search for the Holy Grail."

"I wish you good fortune, Gareth, and that you overcome this knight of the Red Lawns. If you should need aid at any time, I promise I will come if I get word, no matter how distant you may be."

"I know that," said Gareth soberly. So then they sat for many moments each thinking of many things. Until at last it was time for them to separate.

Allan had returned a little while before. He had already heard who the kitchen boy was and how he had been dubbed knight by Sir Launcelot. It had been a day of events for him,

too. Walker, who had made the journey with him had talked
with him of many things.

"This world is large," Walker had said.

"Soon," Allan had said, "I shall go forth and find out for
myself just how large it is."

"Aye, lad," was Walker's reply, "if you travel all the years
you live I doubt if you could see half of it. Far to the south-
east is Rome and there are many lands one must pass before he
reaches there. And to the northeast live the Norse and the
Dane and other tribes equally wild and fierce. Then there
are many seas, which I have heard tell are bigger than the sea
of Cornwall, which I know well. And west of us, there is Ireland and beyond that the world ends."

"Yet shall I go and see what I can. For, if need be I
must go to the very ends of the world and I doubt not it will
be right soon."

"Why, young master?" asked Walker, struck by the se-
riousness of the boy's tone.

But Allan answered not. Nor did the man press his question but watched the lad as he rode on and dreamed.

So they came to the castle. There Yosalinde was awaiting him. Yet after the first greeting, the girl, whose usual contagion of high and gay spirits carried the youth, who was inclined to be more sober minded, along with her, fell into a brown study. Nor would she listen or attend to his attempts to bring her forth into lighter mood. So the boy, a little vexed and nettled, withdrew feeling hurt and gloomy.

But all this was soon swept aside. For Yosalinde came to him and in her eyes was a great light.

"Listen to me, Allan. I had mind made up at first that I would not tell you but have decided otherwise. I too, have dreamed of the Holy Grail. Does it not seem strange that I, a girl, should so do?"

The boy nodded but remained quiet waiting for her to continue.

"You and I are to soon part, Allan. I am to go to a convent where I can bring my mind altogether to the spiritual. I dreamed that when I became worthy I was to help you right well in the finding of it. A spirit will come to me which will guide us both. Think, Allan, if the dream is true, I am to help you and you are to find the Grail."

"So the strange monk told me, Yosalinde. He spoke of one who was to help me and she of whom he spoke, I could not take to be other than you. You and one other and unless I mistake not that other is Sir Launcelot. But it hurts, this thought that you and I will not see each other for the long time you are in the convent."

"But, dear Allan, there is always that time beyond that. It is wonderful to look forward to that, is it not?"

The boy nodded in assent, a little slowly, as if he were realizing that it was so. He looked at the girl now and the feeling grew that Yosalinde was to be the one who would lead him onward. Even now, her fine spirit was helping him to cross the first of the pitfalls. The wish for the girl was the first rung on the high ladder of worthiness.

In the late afternoon the boy returned to the court. Of a truth he had almost forgotten that this was the day for the kitchen boy to come forth. Nor did he, what with thinking of Yosalinde and his mission that must soon be, remember it until he had almost returned.

"Come Walker, let us make haste, for I would know the news."

So they hurried and had not been inside the gates many moments before Allan had found out. But it was only when he came to Sir Launcelot that he heard the other news that he could go forth with the other two on adventure's way.

He was glad that he could go with these two who were also young for he could himself adventure so much the more readily. He would have been abashed to do so with knights such as his own lord or Sir Launcelot and Sir Gawaine.

Sir Launcelot found the boy soon after.

"When you return, and I think it will not be for more than a year, mayhap, two, the King will dub you knight, so I think. Remember Allan, to be worthy for the things ahead and remember, too, that I am at beck and call, if you need me, if so be you can find me.

"This journey will be the great test. I pray that you return and prove what I think you will be. Sir Percival, I understand has armor, sword, lance and spear for you. I shall furnish you with shield. So go you your way and remember that there are few knights who will be found stouter or more skillful than Gareth."

Allan found Gareth soon thereafter and thanked him for letting him go with him. Then did the three, Sir Gareth, Breunor le Noire and Allan plan for many things. The blood of youth raced in their veins even as they planned. Many things would they do. Britain would hear of these three, so they hoped.

A goodly trio, of a truth, they made as they rode forth the next day, the maid Linet with them, and only Walker following behind. Three most worshipful knights watched them as they made their way down the long road and disappeared from view.

Perhaps, too, it was only chance that led them again past the castle of Sir Percival. There Allan made point to enter the same promising to catch up with the others as they continued on their way. Nor could he stay more than but a few moments but in those few moments he had told all to Yosalinde. She, too, watched him, as he hastened to join the others.

Long before he returned she had entered the convent in accordance with the plan of her mother and brother. Yet, in the heart of each of them was only the thought of the future, their hopes were in the far away.

CHAPTER TWENTY

# Gareth Battles Sir Brian

BRAVE and adventurous were the days that followed.
Many days they journeyed to the north. Eager was Sir
Gareth to reach the castle of the fair Dame Lyoness and to
take issue with the Knight of the Red Lawns, her oppressor.

"Yet, good knight," said the fair Lady Linet. "Not
an easy road will you find it. There do be many brave knights
you will find on this road who will seek to joust with you.
Many brave knights who seek adventure as do you."

"If it were not so, then would the way be long indeed.
May such adventure come right soon, we shall welcome it."
So spoke Gareth and his two friends echoed his words.

Yet it was not until the second day that their wish was
fulfilled. For as they rode forward there came a man in great
haste toward them. He further increased his pace and gave
a glad cry of relief.

Said Allan, who was foremost, "What ails you. Why your haste?"

"I have just escaped from some thieves who have entrapped my master. They number six and fierce and sturdy did they seem. I beseech your aid, good masters, for my master is a brave knight who has suffered misfortune."

So then did the three, undecided for the moment, look to each other. Until Breunor le Noire exclaimed.

"Let us to this knight's aid at once." The same thought being in the mind of the other two, they begged the Lady Linet to await them and hurried forward to this, their first adventure.

But the man who came to them, unknowingly, had misled them. For the outlaws numbered more than six as they soon found out. So that when they came to the dell in which the thieves were lodged, the three of them together with Walker, there came forth to oppose them over a dozen ruffians, each carrying either club or mace or spear.

Now did the three give proof of their mettle. Walker, too, wielded a mighty mace that spelled sure death on any of the thieves whom it reached.

[148]

Right skillfully, as if they were veterans, did they hold their place. Right well, they withstood the onslaught of the outlaws and even pressed them back in defense.

A number of the foe had fallen and others uncertain made as if to flee. But they could not go far, for the conquerers, mounted, overtook them. So that there was nothing left for them to do but to turn with their backs to a nearby wall and make a last stand.

Now there were but four of these ruffians left and these threw their arms from them and pleaded mercy. And our youths took heed of their plea and permitted them to escape.

They made rescue of the imprisoned knight who marveled much, after his first expression of gratitude, how so youthful a trio could have overcome the large number of outlaws. Then did he give further proof of his appreciation in that he begged of them that they make his home their abode for that night and he promised them food in plenty and goodly lodging.

Though they were of mind to accept they first besought the wishes of the Lady Linet and she, they found, was not opposed thereto. Right well did they sup then and made them-

selves find comfort before the great fire which blazed merrily. As the night went by, they talked of many things and found their host full of tales of days gone by.

The next morn found them on their way again. Many days they journeyed. Other adventures befell them and in each they accredited themselves right well.

On one of these days, Bruenor le Noire who had speeded ahead so that he was an hour's journey before them had a sad adventure. For as he rode there came toward him an equipage which held many knights and the leader of these was none other than Sir Brian de les Isles.

So as Sir Brian saw him he rode toward him.

"Of what fellowship are you, youth?"

"Of King Arthur's court and it is King Arthur himself who will soon make me his own knight."

"Ill will do I owe this king of yours and all who hold lealty to him. Therefor will I imprison you."

But this they found not quite so easy. Well did the youth oppose them, and many of them suffered thereby. Until there

were those among them who were ready to believe that this was no youth in life but fiend instead.

Yet did he at last succumb because their number was so many. And then did Sir Brian cast him into a prison where Breunor found as many as thirty knights who were prisoners of Sir Brian, some of these were knights of the Round Table.

Soon Gareth and Allan speeded their way to overtake Breunor le Noire of whose absence they began to wonder. Nor did they find trace of him anywhere. Until Allan suggested that they return to the large castle which they had passed, where trace of their comrade might be.

So then did Sir Gareth come to the castle gates; Allan with him. To his beckoning there came forth one of Sir Brian's henchmen.

"Tell your master, Sir Gareth waits outside the gates and would bespeak him."

But when Sir Brian was given the message, he did not deign to answer in person, instead, he sent one of his knights in answer to the call.

"Sir Knight," addressed Sir Gareth, "I seek the master of this castle. Are you he?"

"Nay, but then Sir Brian deems it not fit for him to answer all calls. Such business as you may have, I doubt not, I may quickly dispose with and so not keep you from your journey."

"I seek a youth, companion of ours, who had strayed from us and who mayhap, has met with foul adventure. His name is Breunor le Noire. Do you or the knight who is your master here know aught of him?" So spoke Sir Gareth disdaining the insolence in the tone of the other.

"It may be that we do. Wait you here, while I make return to the castle to find the answer for you."

Therewith the knight left them to stand in front of the castle gates and made his own way back to the house.

"He is an ill bred knave," said Allan hotly. "To think that such as he holds knighthood."

"Knighthood," said the ex-kitchen boy, "is merely a cloak. And I find, Allan, that it is a garment that is only seemly when he who dons it wears it well. Yet this is no time for

anger. Of what matter that this knight is ill bred. If there is any quarrel I shall seek it with his master."

"Think you that they know of his whereabouts?" asked Allan. "I liked not the manner in which he made answer."

"Nor I. But I doubt not we shall know more surely within the next few moments."

Nor did the two have long to wait. For there came from the castle another who seemed to be the high lord. In armor and shield, carrying lance and riding a great black horse, he stood out from among the knights who followed him.

When he came to the gates they were opened wide for him. Then as he saw Sir Gareth and the boy, he made them a sweeping courtesy.

"Forgive our boorishness, Sir Gareth. Pray to enter our humble lodging. Are you then Prince of Orkney?"

"I am so known," replied the young knight. "Yet I seek to be known as Gareth, Knight of the Round Table. I know not your name, Sir Knight, but I find your courtesy welcome."

But now Allan had noted how the knight's manner had

changed. No longer did he seem kindly, instead a dark scowl frowned his face."

"I am Sir Brian de les Isles," was the answer. But the voice was no longer a voice that welcomed, instead it was menacing and stern.

But Sir Gareth seemed to take no note of this. "I seek, Sir Brian, to find a youth who accompanied us. His name is Breunor le Noire, and he seemed to have met with foul adventure."

"Not foul, Sir Gareth, but only such as is meet for all of King Arthur's henchmen."

"Then, I take it, you know of him and of his whereabouts," said Sir Gareth. Still was his manner mild, yet forked lightning seemed to flash from his eyes.

"That we do," replied the other. "He is indeed in safe keeping, such keeping being no other than ours."

"I must trouble you, Sir Knight, to make return of him to us."

"And if I will not?" questioned Sir Brian. Insolence was in his tone, a sneering smile was on his lips.

"I take it, if you will not release him you will fight me as would any honorable knight."

"That will I. Right gladly and to the uttermost, Sir Gareth. For all knights of the Round Table, I am sworn foe."

Then there began a battle such as there was seldom seen. Confidence was in Sir Brian's every move, and truly it would seem that this young knight, still unknown in the field of chivalry, was but a poor adversary to one of the best known of England's knights.

But if Sir Gareth was young, if he was but little known, yet the skill at which Sir Launcelot had marveled, stood him in good stead. This, Sir Brian soon realized. As steel met steel, the older knight knew that his adversary was no mean one.

So they battled for a time. neither of them gaining advantage over the other. Great strength was Sir Brian's, but it was matched by skill and quickness of thrust and parry.

Allan, a lone figure, the only one of the group assembled to stand for Sir Gareth, watched the struggle with bated breath. This boy who had seen men like Sir Launcelot, Sir Tristram, Sir Percival and others of almost equal repute, found his friend

no less able and bold. Clenched were his hands, tense the boyish figure, as with heart and soul afire he watched the two knights.

But soon it became evident that unless untoward happening occurred the outcome of the brave fight was but a matter of time. Slowly, yet surely Sir Brian gave ground. Slowly but surely Sir Gareth pressed him. All the cunning of his foe availed him naught. To the last Sir Brian fought bitterly, silently. His heart held bitterness over the probable outcome, over the youthfulness of the victor to be.

Now as he parried a bold stroke of the other, for each of them had turned to swords long before, there came a flash of steel and Sir Brian felt a great nausea overcome him. Then he knew nothing more for a long time.

He came to later. Eager hands were ministering to him. Feebly he turned, not knowing for the moment why all of this should be. Then his eyes beheld the victor and the boy next to him and he realized what had taken place.

"Sir Gareth," he murmured, as his knights moved aside in response to the weak gesture of his hand, "yours are a victor's spoils. Well have you fought and won."

"Sir Brian," the other replied, "I seek but Breunor le Noire and the release of such knights as you may hold who owe lealty to king Arthur. You are a brave knight, would that your cause were worthy you."

Now Sir Brian called one of his knights to him. The latter followed by Sir Gareth and Allan made their way to the dungeon of the castle. There they found their companion, there too, they found the other knights of the Round Table who had been made prisoners by those within the castle. Great was their joy at release and warmly they thanked their fellow knight.

And now there came a knight to them and told of how well Breunor had fought and what difficulty they had had to make him prisoner.

"If this youth fights but half as well as do the two we have seen, you do indeed make a formidable trio."

Then the three rejoined the Lady Linet and the next morn they were well on their way.

## CHAPTER TWENTY-ONE

# Knight of the Red Lawns

EVENTS followed swiftly thereafter for their journey toward the castle of the Dame Lyoness was not made on easy road. Yet through all these, good fortune stayed with them and so at least they were within a day's journey of their destination.

Word had come to the Red Knight of the Red Lawns of the coming of Sir Gareth. Word too had come to him of the brave deeds of this knight and his two companions. Yet did the Red Knight find naught in it all but cause for great merriment.

"Truly will their courage ooze from them when they behold those many knights hanging from yonder oaks, knights who thought to battle with me and so rescue the Dame Lyoness. Nor did I blame them overmuch, for it is well worth hanging for, perchance to win a smile from so fair a lady. Would that I could be so fortunate."

So said the Red Knight and sighed. No crueler knight

there was in all of Christendom yet was he gentle minded in his love for his fair lady. And though he would not free her of his presence and though he held her closely besieged within the castle, yet had he no desire that harm should come to her.

Now he again made his way to her castle wall where his herald did blow his slughorn and announce that the Red Knight of the Red Lawns besought the light of the lady's countenance and also word with her.

After a due wait there came forth on a balcony within the wall a lady who was indeed beautiful. Straight she held herself, straight and direct her look. Soft brown hair, and her eyes shaded from a dark to lighter brown as they flashed her moods.

Fine was her face, a face of true nobility and gentleness.

And as the Red Knight beheld her, his voice grew gentle, his words strangely softspoken.

"My lady, I am your loyal knight. I pray you to listen to me as I pledge again my loyalty and homage."

There was scorn in the lady's voice, as she cast a withering look upon the knight.

"Soft are your words, Sir Knight. Yet if I do not do the cat a great injustice it is the same softness as is hers when she spies her prey. For yonder I have proof of such knighthood as is yours." And Dame Lyoness pointed to the dead knights hanging from the trees.

"Aye," replied the Red Knight, "and I would go further, I would tear such as would deign to keep me from you, limb from limb. Yet, gentle lady, have I ever shown you proper courtesy and respect as you may well testify. What, I pray you, keeps me from entering this castle now and taking you by force, if need be?"

"My lord," answered Dame Lyoness simply, "that moment you enter these gates I shall drink this brew. A brew that will quickly dispose of all the misery that this earth holds for me. Then will you be able to claim my dead body but naught else. If hope were not mine, if I did not feel certain that some brave knight would come here from King Arthur's court to rescue me from your unwelcome presence, a knight sent here at the beseeching of my sister Linet, I would long ago have drunk this poison and so rid the world of one who has brought naught but misery to many brave knights."

HE KNOCKED WITH THE HILT OF HIS SWORD

"Lady," the Red Knight rejoined, "I hear that such a knight is now on his way. Yet have you overmuch faith in him or mayhap I have given you poor proof of my own skill and strength. If he should come, if his blood does not turn to water, think you he will win from the Red Knight?"

"Yet do I so hope. I pray that he has greater skill and strength than yours. And I shall dare hope."

Then did the lady turn and make her way within, giving the knight no further glance. Ruefully he turned away, and so woeful a figure that few would have known him for the brave and commanding Red Knight of the Red Lawns.

There came the Lady Linet first of all our party of five. She it was who entered the gates of the castle of Dame Lyoness unmolested. So had it been arranged. There she recounted of Sir Gareth and of the others, too. She told of the knight's bravery and how he had overcome Sir Brian de les Isles, and of all their other adventures. Told too, of who Sir Gareth was, and how gentle and how eager he was to take up her gauntlet. Until Dame Lyoness' eyes grew large and their shade dark brown. For she was overly pleased at the description of her champion.

"Yet must he be of the strongest and most skillful," she said fearfully, "to overcome this cruel knight. For the Red Knight is far superior to even Sir Brian."

"Dear Sister," replied Linet, "I have faith in this youthful knight. Naught has he found too difficult as yet and I do not fear the Red Knight whom he meets tomorrow."

So the next morning, Sir Gareth arrived. Awaited him the Red Knight of the Red Lawns who had been advised of his nearness.

As the lady's champion turned with the road, Allan, Breunor and Walker with him, there rode forward to meet him, the knight he was to do battle with.

"What brings you here?" asked the Red Knight, though he knew full well.

"I come to the rescue of Dame Lyoness, who, it seems, is besieged by some unworthy knight who finds it worthy him to war on women."

"I am the Red Knight," the other replied without parley. "See you, my fair knight, yonder trees. See you the things

that hang therefrom. They are the bodies of such other fools who have come here to teach me what I may or may not do."

"That, too," replied Sir Gareth, "makes me but doubly certain that knighthood is not the garment you should wear. I shall do battle with you, Sir Knight, so soon as you don armor. Meantime I await your pleasure."

Then did the three ride toward the castle. And as they neared it there came to the open window both the Lady Linet and the Dame Lyoness. Low did the latter courtesy to them all, but chiefest to Sir Gareth. Long did these two gaze at each other and in that gaze love was in the dawning.

Now, the Red Knight came forward. For a few moments each watched the other, their horses stepping now this way, now that. Then of a sudden, they made at each other, with all their might. And well it was that shields were there to meet the blows. For such was their force that breast plates, horsegirths and cruppers burst. Both knights were sent to earth, Sir Gareth holding the reins of his bridle still in his hands. Sore stunned was each for many minutes. Wonder it was that neck of either was not broken.

Now the two left their horses and with shields in front they

[163]

battled with their swords. And they fought until midday **and**
until they both lacked wind. So that each was forced to **take**
rest.

From their window, the two ladies watched the affray.
Both of them prayed that harm should not come to their champion.

But the Red Knight watching them and seeing how in
especial Dame Lyoness was interested, conceived a new idea.

"I fancy that when I overcome this knight and prepare to
hang him, yonder good lady will give herself to me to save him.
For she seems to care overmuch for him and greatly do I wish
I were in his place. Yet must she be the lady of the Red
Knight." So he mused.

They fought all of the afternoon. Now one would grovel
in the earth, the other too weak to carry the battle to successful
conclusion, now the second would grow equally weak.

Then did they rest again and Breunor and Allan brought
water for Sir Gareth so that he could drink and bathe his face.
They rested for a half hour and then battled once again.

**Now the** younger knight seemed weaker. **The Red**

Knight pressed him hard as he saw this. Things began to look dark for the lady's champion.

She, too, saw this. And coming far to the edge of the balcony she called out.

"Sir Gareth, I pray for your success." And as he looked toward her there was a great, eager light on her countenance. It gave to him renewed strength, renewed faith. As if he had ten men's strength. And so he turned on the Red Knight and the other could not withstay him. Fearfully he struck him, such a fearful blow that the Red Knight never moved again. Yet even as his foe succumbed, the victor slowly crumbled to the ground, spent and so weak that for a few seconds Allan, Breunor le Noire and the two ladies who had hurried to him, thought he was dead.

In a few moments however the young knight opened his eyes. Then, beholding the gentle face of Dame Lyoness, he closed them again, well content.

## CHAPTER TWENTY-TWO

# Sir Galahad

OF THE things that befell Sir Gareth, of how he wedded the good Dame Lyoness and of how he gave right seemly proof of his worship, this story will not detail. Nor can we go on the byway that deals with the deeds of Breunor le Noire who was made a knight of the Round Table by King Arthur soon thereafter and who then avenged the cowardly slaying of his father by the unknown and false knight.

For our tale must hold its course hereafter. The boy Allan had grown with the two years that had passed since the adventure of the Red Knight of the Red Lawns. He had not returned to the court of King Arthur, instead he and Walker had set out on journey of adventure. No hit and miss journey this, instead it followed a call that the boy had had, a call which he knew meant that the time had come for him to begin seeking the Holy Grail.

The two years had been eventful ones for Allan. All over

England had he found his way, he and Walker. Adventures were many and everywhere this youth through kindly deeds and brave actions left good repute behind him.

So at the period which our narrative now covers there had grown from a whispering into a more or less certainty and belief that a man had come who would find the Holy Grail again for Britain and so add honor and fame to England. And therewith there was great wonderment as to whether the finder would be of the court of Northgalis, or of Northumberland, or of Cornwall, or of Arthur's court.

Pentecost was but a few days away. Now on this day the good King Arthur with Launcelot, Percival and Merlin, the wizard, made the round of the sieges or seats of the Round Table, each of which held a name, for on this Pentecost to come, there were to be many new knights made and place must be found for them.

So then here and there the places were assigned. Now they came to the last of the places.

"What new knight shall be placed here?" asked the King. "It seems to us that this place has been empty this long time."

"This," answered Merlin, "is the Siege Perilous. Here no one shall sit until four hundred and fifty four years after the passion of the Lord."

Now then Sir Launcelot make quick reckoning.

"In the name of God," he made haste to say, "then should this siege be filled on this Pentecost day that comes."

"That I doubt not," replied Merlin. "And no one else but the rightful occupant may fill it for he that is so hardy as to try it, he will be destroyed."

So Pentecost day came. And all but Merlin wondered as to who the newcomer, who would fill this seat could be.

Early day found the new knights already seated. Early day, too, found Allan, once again, after the many months away from the court, returned. This was home to him—and close to three years had passed since he had been there. He had learned much, he had searched thus far in vain for the Holy Grail. Yet not altogether in vain, for he felt within him that he was closer to his quest with the passing of each day. The boy, now in young manhood, had indeed developed well. Broad shouldered, slim-waisted, supple limbed, he gave little indication of

A SOLITARY HORSEMAN

his strength, yet Walker riding close beside him, had watched him, had trained him and had with great pride, noted his skill with lance, sword and spear. Well he knew that this youth would soon be second to none in ability to cope with foe or in friendly jousting as might befall in tournament or elsewhere.

Now on this Pentecost day, Allan had returned because it was wont that he should do so and also because desire urged him thence. So then he entered the great hall and because all of King Arthur's court were within, none there were who knew him.

And once he found himself within, only Merlin the Wizard knew who he was. The others knew him not, not even Sir Percival nor Sir Launcelot. So Merlin came forward and greeted him.

"They do not yet know you lad, for greatly have you changed with these few years. Almost grown to full manhood and of a truth full well and ready for the further conduct of your mission. Come you with me for your seat is saved."

"Nay, sir, I hold no seat for I am as yet no knight, though hopeful," replied the lad.

"Yet is your place here, lad.   So come."

And herewith the lad had need to follow.   While all about, the knights and others watched them both.

So now as they came to the Siege Perilous, Merlin stopped and motioned Allan toward it.   Yet the boy hesitated and turned his eyes to his king, whose eyes searched both the Wizard and the boy.

Thereupon Merlin turned to them all.

"Here is Galahad, he who shall achieve the Grail.   And proof of it is in this that he shall sit in the Siege Perilous and no harm shall come to him therewith.   Sit you down, lad."

So Allan sat down in the place assigned.   There seemed to play about him and the seat a strange light.   Well he seemed to fit therein.

"Oh, King," went on Merlin.   "Some years since, there came a stranger to this youth and also to one other here.   There and then he declared that the finding of the Grail was made possible.   That the finder was to be known as Galahad the Chaste.   Pure and upright must the seeker be and up to now there is none other among you who so well fills this requirement.

In the Court of King Arthur

He who left here as Allan, page to Sir Percival, returns, fitted and grown to the task. He shall henceward be known as Galahad. And it please you sire, make you him a knight of the Round Table. So that if he do find the Grail, honor and glory shall be with you, too."

Wondered the boy yet, but at word from the king he came forward and knelt.

"We dub you knight, Allan. You shall be known as Sir Galahad. Fruitful may your mission be. We know that knighthood shall not suffer through you."

A little apart, Sir Launcelot watched the boy. And though the newly made knight knew it not, the former had watched him through the many days he had been away from the court, had never been very far, yet never so near that the young adventurer knew it. Most keen and watchful had he been to see that the lad kept on the clean road ahead. And of a truth he had noted, with a restful content, that such was the boy's inclination and desires. Yet he kept apart even as he watched and in all the years had not come face to face with the boy.

## CHAPTER TWENTY-THREE

# The Beginning of the Quest

A WEEK and a day Sir Galahad stayed at the court. Nor was he there many hours before he found that Yosalinde was not home as yet but would be within the month. Yet he would not stay, for after long and serious converse with both Merlin and Sir Launcelot, he followed the great urge to go forward. For he felt the call now greater, more insistent. Yet did he somewhat fret since this urge, this call seemed to lead him nowhere, seemed only to beckon that he go.

"Fret not, lad, perhaps many a year shall you wander before you find the Grail. Many places shall you go. Yet let not your way ever be impatient." So spoke the Wizard.

"I go to Normandy soon, Merlin."

"You shall find me there," now spoke Sir Launcelot, "for I too go hither to seek adventure. I pray that we meet, Galahad and that together we have many eventful days. Though full well do I know your way in great part, must be alone."

"That it must be," Merlin advised.

And so the next day and the next he stayed. From everyone and everywhere great favor was his. King Arthur, too, held much converse with him and he remembered the first days the lad had come to court and how he had ordered the herald to send him forth for Sir Launcelot and Gawaine.

But the day came at last when he and Walker adventured forth. And the new knight carried no shield for one was awaiting him, a shield that carried a great cross to signify his seeking. This he was to find at the convent near Carboneck. So Merlin had advised him.

Two days of journey passed without ontoward event but on the third day there came to him a yeoman in great woe.

"What grieves you, friend?" asked Walker while Sir Galahad waited.

"Great are my troubles for my master will surely flay me until I die. I was bringing him his best horse from the castle when a knight stopped me. Though I told him that the horse was my master's and how much store he set by it yet did he take the same from me. When I protested as best I might, he

brought his sword upon me and it was fortune that I was not slain."

"Know you the knight?" asked Sir Galahad kindly.

"Nay, Sir, except that he told me he needed the horse at Calomet."

"I shall go hither. It is but a short journey and you may come with me. For it does not seem a knightly act, this taking of your master's horse and it needs explaining."

"I thank you master. For little value though my life may be, I value it nevertheless," replied the yeoman.

So they went on to Calomet. And when they arrived there the yeoman most fortunately espied his master's horse.

"Yonder, Sir Knight, is the horse," and he pointed excitedly.

There stood a white horse, truly a beast well worth owning. A beautiful head, a great body that showed strength and grace, set well on strong, shapely limbs. A head which its owner held right fearlessly, yet the eyes of the beast were soft and kindly and indicated that he could be ridden by child or woman.

"A good beast and well worth fighting for, if need be," said Walker.

"Yet more worthy the fight, if there is need of one, the fact that this knight we are to meet is so unfair," replied Sir Galahad.

So now they came to the house. Walker and the yeoman dismounted and went up to the horse, which had been tied but temporarily and was awaiting its rider.

And as they stood there, there came from within the house a knight who had espied them.

"What wish you, knaves?" he asked, scowling.

"It is my master who wishes your presence," replied Walker.

"He shall have his wish satisfied," the knight made reply, turning to Galahad, who was a little further away.

"Do you wish word with me, Sir Knight?" he asked.

"I seek him who claims to be the owner of this horse," replied Sir Galahad.

"Then you have found him for he is no other than I," was the answer.

"Yet how can he be yours, Sir Knight, if this yeoman claims it is his master's horse?" Sir Galahad questioned.

"I have made you answer to question that should concern you but little. What ado wish you to make of it?"

"Only that the horse goes to this yeoman so that he can bring him to his rightful owner."

The other laughed aloud.

"I wot, strange knight, I wonder well how you can do this thing when I am here to say you nay. And when my sword is even more severe in keeping you from boastful attempt."

And then without further parley the knight brought his sword to play. But sorry adventure this for him and Sir Galahad though still without shield brought him right quickly to earth. A sorry match was he for the young knight, so ill matched that Walker smiled in glee at his efforts.

The knight now held his peace as Sir Galahad told the yeoman to take his master's horse and go hence. But he scowled and as Sir Galahad turned to go he bespoke him.

"Sir Knight, I shall not forget your meddling in what was

SIR GALAHAD IN THE FOREST

of no concern to you.   And the day may come when you will regret this deed."

"True, Sir Knight," replied Sir Galahad.   I shall have need to make assurance that my horse is secured so that he may not be stolen."   And laughing and full at ease he left the beaten knight to his surly thoughts.

Yet as he went the strange yeoman followed him.   So that Sir Galahad turned to him somewhat in amaze.

"I thought that your way was opposite."

"My way, Sir Knight, goes only to yonder turn.   Yet before I leave I make you gift of this horse.   He is yours.   That was not a true tale as to who owned this horse.   For its true owner is none other than you and my story such as to test you and find answer to whether you would help those who are in trouble, though the trouble owner be lowly born.   The horse is sent by friend of yours whose name is not to be related.   I wish you well, Sir Knight."

Much overcome was Sir Galahad at the princely gift, for the horse had impressed him much.

"Tell you this unknown friend of mine, that I value this

gift as naught else.   Tell you too, that I name him the Seeker, in full honor of my quest."

So then the strange yeoman departed whilst the knight and his faithful man went on their way.

## CHAPTER TWENTY-FOUR

# In Normandy

OF THE travels of Sir Galahad, of how he journeyed through many lands and new scenes, there is much to be told. Ever with him, went his faithful man, Walker, who served him well and loyally.

Eager was the young knight to reach Normandy of which he had heard much. So he sailed away and since many rumors held the Grail to be there he hoped to find it.

In Normandy, a strange land, he met with much adventure, many knights brave and true, and some who were not. But no sign of the Grail was there to be had.

On his white horse, the Seeker, he made his way southward, finding lodging where he could.

It was so, in the first month of his travels, that he came to the castle of one of the best of Normandy's knights. Of him, Sir Launcelot had spoken highly; he held him in great

esteem, and so had counseled the youthful knight to make it his purpose to visit him when there.

Sir Guilbert gave him friendly greeting. Many had been his visits to England, well he knew Sir Launcelot and Sir Percival and the great King himself. Sir Galahad found his stay a pleasant one; there were friendly jousts in which he met some of Normandy's worshipful knights. In all of these he was victor.

Sir Guilbert had full praise for the young knight. There was son of his, a youth of seventeen, who also admired the new-comer, even as Allan the boy had admired Sir Launcelot. When his visitor's stay was drawing to a close, Sir Guilbert spoke of this.

"My son Charles, Sir Galahad, has taken great fancy to you and wishful am I that you could find it in your plans to take him as page. He is a quiet lad, sturdy and obedient, you will find. And following wish of his mother, he knows your English tongue well, for she is Englishborn. He has made study of Latin too, it seemed for a time that he would turn to priesthood. But that will not be, and I cannot say that it finds me regretful. I would have him a true knight, had I my way."

"Your wish, Sir Guilbert, may well be served. But if I may, I should like first to speak to the lad, before I make answer."

"Faith, and you may. For we should want the lad to satisfy you and merit your friendship. I shall see to it that you have the chance to speak with him. It were better, that he know not the reason for your questioning. Is it not so?"

"It would be best, Sir Guilbert," Sir Galahad replied.

Then the two talked of other things and the young knight questioned his friend as to the likely whereabouts of the Holy Grail.

"Many rumors have I heard, Sir Galahad. But never actual trace. Understand you well, my friend. Knights from every land seek this Grail and I would wish that it were Norman who found it. But if it cannot be one from my own land, I would it were one from your country. I fear me, it shall not be easy search, it may lead you far."

"I am well prepared for that," replied the Seeker. "If it were easy to find, the glory would be so much the less. I can but hope that I shall have the vision to see it when it is near me."

[181]

"I wish you well," Sir Guilbert made answer. "Now let us repair to the dining hall for the meal waits."

It was after they had eaten that Sir Galahad found the opportunity to hold speech with the youth, Charles.

He found the lad to be all that his father had said of him.

"What have you wish for, Charles?" he said.

"I should like to journey far and to many places," the boy replied. "There is much to see and I envy the many who have traveled to foreign lands."

"How then, if you could, would you travel?"

"As a true Norman knight serving God and the Church against all infidels."

"Well spoken, lad. But it needs many years and one must learn much to be a good knight. It is not easy work."

"I know that, Sir Galahad. But I shall not count the years for I am still young."

More questions the knight asked the lad and he made eager though respectful answer. It was apparent that he had thought of it for many a day. But Sir Galahad said never a

word to him of the reason for his questions and left the lad without knowledge of his purpose.

But the next day he spoke to Sir Guilbert and gave him answer.

"I should like the youth as my page. He is the kind I could well use. And I promise you that he shall come back to you so that neither you nor his mother shall have reason to be other than proud of him. He will be of great help to me when I reach Rome for I purpose to journey there. I know nought of the tongue."

"Have you told the lad, as yet?" the father asked.

"I thought it best that either you or your lady speak first with him and then will I."

"That is a gracious deed on your part, my knight. And if it bears fruit or not, I shall indeed be in your debt."

"Not so, Sir Guilbert. For the boy will but have such chance as I was given by Sir Percival when I was even younger than he."

## CHAPTER TWENTY-FIVE

# Sir Galahad Offers Help

IT WAS but a week and a day later that Sir Galahad proceeded further. With him was the faithful Walker who was overly pleased to be on his way and also Charles, the young son of Sir Guilbert. Eager was the lad and highly pleased to go forth with the brave knight.

Sir Galahad had had hopes of meeting Sir Launcelot who had planned to be in Normandy, and Merlin as well. But he would wait no longer, he was in no mood to tarry now.

There came a day of storm, fierce was the rain and sleet and the wind so strong that the knight, and his party found it arduous task to keep the road. Sir Galahad decided to stop and seek shelter at the first refuge that they should find.

A little later they came to an old but magnificient castle and in answer to the summons of Walker, an ancient man appeared.

"What will you?" the old man quavered.

"My master seeks shelter until the storm passes. He is a worshipful knight. Go you to your master with his request."

The man hobbled within the castle. Soon he returned.

"There is no master here but my mistress bids me welcome the worshipful knight and beseech his entrance."

So they went within and the old man threw logs on the open fire which blazed right merrily. Sir Galahad and the two with him made themselves comfortable. Soon food and drink was brought to them of which they partook with good grace.

The storm did not subside and night came on.

"Old man," Sir Galahad said to the ancient servitor. "Pay you my respects to the lady whose hospitality we enjoy and ask that she grace us with her presence. Tell her that it is Sir Galahad, Knight of the Round Table, who seeks it."

There came a long wait which left the three a wondering. Then there came forth a lady who was followed by the ancient servitor. Stately she was and of noble bearing. Yet it could be seen that she was fearful and disturbed.

[185]

"My lord wished my presence?" she asked and her tone was tremulous.

"I owe you apology for this disturbance," the knight said courteously. "But we also owe you thanks for your gracious hospitality. There seems need that we disturb you further since the storm stays and we cannot proceed as we would. May we find lodging within your walls?"

The lady looked fearfully about.

"I cannot deny you. Truly it is no night to be outdoors. Stay then and welcome."

Morning found the storm in no wise abated. The lady of the castle did not appear at the morning meal. But the old man was there to serve them. He too, seemed much disturbed and made as if to have speech with Sir Galahad, once or twice.

"What troubles your pate, old man?" Walker finally asked him.

"These are dark days for the house of Sanscourt," the latter replied and crossed himself.

"Perhaps, good man, it may be within us to lighten them,"

Sir Galahad said kindly, "If we can, it may repay in part for your mistress' hospitality."

"Would that my lady could find it in her to confide in you. For you seem right friendly, my lord."

"Beseech you her. Tell her that Sir Galahad offers his services if she has need of them."

The man soon returned.

"My lady thanks you kindly for your offer and she will see you soon," he said.

The Knight waited but a few moments when his hostess came into the room.

"You are gracious, Sir Galahad. I doubt whether there can be any help for me. Yet I shall tell you my story for there still may be hope for so wretched a person as myself."

"My lady, it is the duty of all true knights to be of help to those in distress. Wherefore, I hold but to my knightly vow, in my promise of service to you."

The Lady Jeanne made no answer, seemingly she had not heard him. Sir Galahad watched her, saw her look which

seemed afar, saw the dark rims around her eyes. They spoke of many hours of weeping.

Now she turned to him.

"I think, my lord, this storm that seems as if it will not cease has been sent by God. Strange though it may seem it brings me hope, dim though that hope may be, yet I treasure it. Little reason for hope have I had.

"Think me not rude, Sir Galahad, and think not that I question your valor or skill. But this is task for no lone knight, for my enemy is strong and powerful. I may be selfish too, in that I draw you into my troubles but I am like one who drowning, must need snatch at a straw. And many knights would hesitate long to offer service where the cause is as hopeless as mine seemingly is. Nor will I blame you or hold you, if after my story is done, you find no way in which you can help me.

"Listen then and you will see why I count this storm as sign of hope sent to me."

## CHAPTER TWENTY-SIX

# Lady Jeanne's Story

"TWO years will it be next month when the Duke of Gascony with fifty knights went forth on a quest that would take them to far Eastern lands. Of these fifty, Sir Vilard, my husband, was one.

"He left with me, my son Ambrose, my daughter Helene and two servitors, old men who could not go with him. It was in a good and holy cause so I had no tears for him to see. Rather did I bid him Godspeed and a safe and quick return.

"You see me alone now. Two years, and I have neither son, nor daughter, nor husband. Did I know they were dead, bitter would be my woe yet would I count God's mercies many, His ways strange, but not for any mortal to question. But I do not know that. They would have me believe my husband dead. Ambrose went forth one day and I have had no word of him since then. And my daughter is lodged within prison walls waiting the whim of Sir Dolphus who holds her in his power.

[189]

"They tell me that my husband perished with the Duke and all but three of the knights that went forth with him. And that before he died he sent word that it was his wish that I permit Sir Dolphus to marry our daughter. Yet do I know that Sir Dolphus is already lawfully wedded to a wife whom he would discard. Knowing my husband as I do, I could not believe such to be his message. So I withstood the pleadings of this knight until his pleadings turned to bitter threats.

"He would make himself Duke of Gascony. And when I would not listen to him, his pleadings or threats, he came here one day with two other knights and professed to abide by such decision as I had made. They dined with us. Ambrose, my son, was away that day.

"Enough to say that they stole my daughter from me. This old man you see and the other, Albert, were clubbed to earth, the one to death. I tried so hard to resist them but my hand was weak.

"When Ambrose returned, I could not keep him. He went forth to rescue his sister. Poor lad, I have had no word from him since then. Is he dead? Did they kill him? I have sent for word, have begged that they tell me what fate has befallen him but they profess not to know.

"I have heard that the Church will not sanction his marriage to Helene. Nor will it permit Sir Dolphus to annul the marriage with his wife. A good priest also tells me that Sir Dolphus has set his black heart upon marrying my poor Helene so that he can then lawfully own all this land and estate that belongs to us. It will be small matter to rid himself of me and I fain would not wish to live were it not that I still have hope.

"My lord, I have hoped so much. Until my very hope turned black for never was there any one so helpless against the power of this wicked man. I dread the coming of each day and yet mixed with my dread there still is ever present that one small hope which will not be killed.

"I think I would have died but for this small hope," she added wistfully. She paused now and seemed lost in the dark thoughts that possessed her.

"All of them gone. Not one of them to remain with me."

"Sir Galahad," she turned to him. "It is not a pretty story. I seem to be encompassed with tragedy. I would not include you in my woes, you have other missions, other work

ahead. And though you have the valor and strength of ten, it would count for so little."

"My lady," the knight replied. "What use would such valor be, if I had it, if I did not but use it for its full worth? Could I be a true knight and not heed the call your sorrow brings? I can but try to help you. And that, I swear, I will."

A light shone in the lady's eye. "I was not wrong to hope. Even now I feel that succor must come. Your words, dear knight, give me strength. Surely then, the storm has brought me some ray of that hope I speak of."

"I shall devise some plan," Sir Galahad said, "wherein we can make rescue of your daughter, and find out the fate of your son."

The Knight's thoughts were deep for many minutes. "Did this Sir Dolphus say where your husband met his death?"

"Near Lombardy," she replied.

"If I succeed here, my lady, I shall continue my way to Rome. From there I shall journey north and seek news of your husband. It may be that he is not dead. Dead or alive, you at least will know.

"Tomorrow, if the day clears, we shall turn to the work before us. It seems a hard task but as I have said, we can but try. In the meantime, my Lady Jeanne, have courage and keep your patience."

So Galahad left her. But Walker stayed.

"Lady, I would but add my humble word of cheer. In all of England, of all the Knights of the Round Table, there is none who equals my master in skill and bravery. I tell you this so that you may know how worthy your champion is. Would that he had but one other with him and I would not care what odds were against him."

"And who, my man, is that other?"

"Sir Launcelot," Walker made reply.

"I thank you for telling me of Sir Galahad. It adds to the hope I have and the courage he bids me possess."

## CHAPTER TWENTY-SEVEN

# Sir Launcelot Arrives

THE day dawned bright and clear. But it brought to Sir Galahad no plan for the rescue of the daughter of his hostess.

My lady came down to the breakfast table greatly cheered, as was plain to be seen. Sir Galahad had not the heart to tell her that as yet he had found no way for the rescue of her daughter. Instead he said.

"It seems to me that there is one thing I can but do. I shall seek this knight's castle and wait for such event there as may befall. Luck may come my way. But I promise you this, my lady, I shall make no rash or fruitless attempt at rescue. Rash acts may well come after the rescue of your daughter, not before."

The Lady Jeanne agreed. So then immediately after the meal Walker, and the page Charles prepared the things they would need for the journey.

"I go forth to prepare the horses, young master. Will you see to these things here?" So spoke Walker and when Charles agreed he hurried outdoors.

SUDDENLY THEY MADE FOR EACH OTHER

Hardly had he reached there, however, when he saw two horsemen coming toward him. His trained eye easily recognized them. One could be no other than Sir Launcelot. Only he sat his horse so. And the rider with him was Gouvernail, he who had been squire to Sir Tristram until that brave knight had died and who now was in the service of Sir Launcelot.

"By my faith," spoke out Walker to the empty air. He rubbed his eyes. Yes, it was they.

"A wish come true," was all he could think of. And then he danced first on one foot, then on the other, uncertain whether to rush to meet the advancing horsemen or to run inside and advise his master. His uncertainty ended only when he was indoors again.

"Master, master, come you here," he called. "See who comes," he shouted gleefully.

Sir Galahad came toward him. But not as quick as the eager, youthful Charles. After them all, came the Lady Jeanne.

"It is Launcelot, by my faith," Sir Galahad shouted gleefully. He was to meet me in Normandy and has followed close on my heels. What luck!" And he waved to the ap-

proaching knight who returned the salute and increased his speed.

The Lady Jeanne turned questioning eyes to the squire, who nodded happily.

"My lady," Sir Galahad turned to her. "Now you may well have hope and faith. And well may you give us your blessing for we shall bring your daughter to you, have no fear."

So spoke the knight whose faith in Sir Launcelot's prowess was most profound.

Now the approaching knight came up to them.

"Good Allan," he said still calling his friend by the name of his boyhood. "I have traveled through a day of storm to catch up with you. Until I am sure that this knave here is prepared to seek a master who would be saner and more considerate."

"Not so," replied Gouvernail, "for I was no less the anxious."

"You come in good time, dear friend. For never were you more needed. There is work ahead for us, serious work. This lady here needs our help. She is sore distressed. But let her meet you."

So the Lady Jeanne met Sir Launcelot. And once again the tale of her plight was revealed. And even as Sir Launcelot listened, the plan of what to do came to Sir Galahad. But he kept his tongue until his friend was fully informed and had in turn had time to question their hostess.

Charles stood close to his master, whose arm encircled him as if it would include him in all of it. A little in the background stood the two squires who were close friends and old comrades. Gouvernail's interest was keen.

So when the tale was done, Sir Galahad turned to his friend and said "Know you perchance where Merlin is?"

"We left him behind us. His old bones could not risk yesterday's storm. But he promised me that he would follow when it cleared and so he is but a day behind. But have you a plan, Allan?"

"It has but just come to me—this possible plan. It may be that he can be emissary from Arthur to the Duke of Gascony for such purpose as may be devised. And we go with him as knights. We *know not,* of course, that a pretender sits where the Duke of Gascony should. And I fancy that this Dolphus will be right well pleased to welcome us and if we seemingly appear not too scrupulous ourselves we can worm the story from him and act thereon."

"It can be done, if the plan is well thought out. Only dear lad, I doubt whether thy face will not count against you in any pretended villainy. Think you not so, madame?"

The Lady Jeanne smiled. It was strange to see her smile but it gave proof that she was lighter hearted.

"I think that Sir Dolphus is not the kind to think that there are any who hold aught but villianous thoughts," she replied.

"So then, we must need delay until Merlin comes."

"Think you the king will be provoked at our use of him and his court?" Sir Galahad asked.

"Aye, that I do. Provoked that he was not with us to share in the adventure." Launcelot laughingly replied.

"Lady," Sir Launcelot addressed her in a moment's pause "You had little need to worry when this knight became your champion. He is overly modest. Gladly shall I help him."

"God is good," the Lady Jeanne replied brokenly. "And He has placed me and my troubles in godly hands." And then she wept. And it seemed as if like a spring freshet, her thoughts, soul, and heart, were cleared and cleansed.

# CHAPTER TWENTY-EIGHT

# A Rescue

"I SEEK speech with him who is Duke of Gascony. I bring him a message from Arthur, King of England." So spoke Merlin as he stood at the entrance of the great and splendid castle of the ruler of Gascony.

By his side were the two knights, Galahad and Launcelot. The page Charles stood close by and somewhat behind them were the two squires, Walker and Governail.

"From England's king? the Gascon knight questioned. And made as if he would further satisfy his curiosity. But changed his mind.

"I pray you wait, good sir, until I tell my lord, your message." So then he went within the great hall.

"A rash adventure, say I," and Merlin shook his head dolefully.

"You were ever a croaker, good Merlin," replied Sir Launcelot. "See not the thing so dolefully, I pray you."

"And think of the worth of what we accomplish," added Sir Galahad. "Here now comes the Gascon with his answer, I see." Let us listen to what he says.

"We bid you welcome to Gascony and pray you to come within. My master sends his greetings and awaits you."

They followed then their guide and so came within the great hall of state where Sir Dolphus awaited them.

"Come you from England?" he asked.

"That we do," replied Merlin, "and carry a message for the Duke."

"There is no Duke of Gascony. He is dead. But I, by the will of all the nobles of the land, rule in place. If you have message from England's king honor is mine to receive it."

"That message will I deliver right gladly. My king has long desired to come to Gascony and to other countries in France. So has he sent me forth to find first, how welcome will his visit be, second, as you may well understand, that such country as may come within his plans may worthy be his presence. For England's king must hold his honor and his **presence** at their royal worth.

"So come I to this brave land the which my king has heard well spoken and which he holds in high esteem. I find it sad news that he who reigned is dead, yet Gascony cannot suffer if you, most worshipful sir, rule instead."

Now did the crafty Dolphus find himself quick to see the worth to him of such a visit from the great king of England who was held in high esteem everywhere. If Arthur were to visit him then could none question his pretense to the throne. Too, were such visit soon, there would be need for him to be declared Duke of Gascony at once, so that Arthur could be met in royal state.

"Gascony, good sir, would welcome your king. And count it honor to receive him with all the honors due so great a name. When does your master plan to come?"

"Shortly, sir, after I make my return to England and make report. For he hopes also to visit Rome and pay homage to His Holiness, the Pope.

When he heard this, Sir Dolphus urged the emissaries of England's king to tarry awhile in Gascony.

"So that, kind sirs, you find our friendship for your master, such as may befit his visit to us. Greatly do we desire him to come and we would wish your report to be a kindly one. So find you welcome here. We shall eat, drink and be merry."

So the party made itself at home. Sir Dolphus soon took great fancy to Sir Launcelot who proved a merry soul and the two spent many hours together.

"I would count it fortunate, Sir Launcelot, were you knight of this court. For I need friends such as you."

"Rather, I fancy, is the need otherwise. For the Duke of Gascony's friendship is no small thing and many there are who would hold it high honor. Of friends, you should have many." So the knight made flattering answer.

"Aye, but you know not. There are those who would believe that the dead duke lives and who though silent, yet are sullen over my rightful claim to take his place. And I find the Church of little help to me. Though I have offered it many gifts, and promised it great riches, yet will it oppose my will."

"Does the Church object to you as Duke?" Sir Launcelot questioned. "I see not why."

[202]

"Nay, 'tis not as Duke but in other matters."

Caution seemed to overcome Sir Dolphus for many minutes. But he had great desire to confide in this friendly knight whose good will he wished.

"Art thou married, Sir Launcelot?" he asked.

"A strange question, my friend. Yet do I find my happiness in the single blessedness which is at present mine."

"Yet is marriage a most convenient thing sometime. 'Twould be for me at present."

"Say you, 'twould be? Yet, if I mistake not, have I heard that that blessed state is already yours. Though no sign have I seen as yet, of the Lady Dolphus.

"Aye, friend, married am I, worse the pity. And when I ask the Church to annul this unhappy state, and give it many gifts, still does it turn stubborn over such a little thing."

"What harm therein, my friend? Since that the lady is not with you?" Friendly was Sir Launcelot's tone and right sympathetic.

"Aye, there I come back to what I have said—about

marriage being most convenient at times. For would they annul the marriage I could then marry again, one who owns vast estate. And that would make me all powerful in Gascony."

Such laughter as shook the frame of Sir Launcelot. Nor was it unkindly.

"A great rogue you," he spoke pleasantly. "Off with the old and on with the new. Is it not so? And I fancy the new is also right young or I am greatly mistaken? Eh?

Great was Sir Launcelot's hilarity. Nor did the other take offense thereat.

"I care little as to her youth or not. But I do care for the estate that goes with her," replied Sir Dolphus.

"She must like you greatly, to be willing?"

"Hardly could I say, she's that. But that would be small matter if I could but get the Church to sanction the deed. Yet have I hope that if I could get your king's goodwill, he could persuade the Pope on his visit to Rome. And there, good friend, you could help me greatly and well would I repay such kindness."

Not once did Sir Launcelot permit the hot temper within him to be unloosed. Played he so well with the wicked knight that it was but a few days thereafter Sir Dolphus invited him to visit with him the young damsel who was kept within prison walls. Never once did the knight demur or permit the other to think that he did not sympathize and agree with his plans.

As they walked away from the prison door, he turned to the other. "Strange that she should be all alone. Has she no one who would make you trouble?"

"Her father went forth with the Duke and others among us to the land of the infidels. On our way back, in Lombardy, our small force was overcome by disaster. But three of us escaped, I know not what happened to the others. Then it was, I decided to possess the land of the Sanscourt and told the Lady Jeanne that her husband wished and commanded that her daughter Helene marry me. But she would have none of this. So that I had to steal the damsel. And when her brother came here to rescue her, we overcame the helpless youth. He would not have lived had I my way, but the others would not permit that and so we have him safely lodged in the dungeon below and I fancy he will not abuse our hospitality for long."

That night Sir Launcelot spoke to the others and told what he had heard. Great was his rage, which he had curbed so well when in the presence of the other.

"I would," Merlin spoke in great gloom, "that we were well out of this."

"We can be well out of it when the youth and girl are also safely out," Sir Galahad replied and there was a stern look in his eye. "Tomorrow we shall find the dungeon place. Then will we act quickly. But also we must see to it that this false knight receives his just deserts. Is it not so, Launcelot?"

"Tomorrow, it shall be," the other replied. "And I myself, shall deal with this Sir Dolphus, for I have had to listen to his foulness without demur."

So they planned. And the next day, Sir Galahad professed a great desire to see the whole of the castle. And so was shown in due course the great dungeon and saw there, the weak and spent lad, Ambrose.

That night, Sir Dolphus and Sir Launcelot went by themselves to the chamber of the former to make merry. And there, Sir Dolphus who counted the other's sympathy as beyond

doubt, told more of his knavish plots.   Until the listener sick
with listening turned to him in the quiet and secrecy of the great
chamber and said in stern tones.

"Sir Dolphus, I would advise you to pray now.   For you
die in three minutes!"

Nor did the other mistake the voice, the tone.   Nor even
make pretense to misunderstand.   Instead he made as if to
raise a great shout.   But found the other's mighty hand closed
over his foul mouth so that his call for aid was unuttered.   And
the hand remained there—even as the owner forced him to his
knees with no great effort.

"Pray, if you will.   Your time is almost gone."

But the wretch groaned and squirmed and tried to escape
the hold that held viselike over him.

It was five minutes later that Sir Launcelot left the room.
There was a grim, fixed look on his face that few had ever seen
before.

He joined the others.   And then while and Gouvernail
went to the prison chamber of the damsel, Helene, and rescued
her with little effort, Sir Galahad went down to the dungeon

door and there overcame the guard with ease and opened the door wide with the keys obtained. And Walker carried the weak lad to the entrance door and so they joined the others.

So then Sir Galahad and Sir Launcelot with the two squires went for and obtained their horses, without suspicion. With the two they had rescued, the whole party rode forth from the castle. And but for the outcry of the guards at the gate which they forced them to open wide, they had no one to cope with.

Forth they road swiftly, Merlin carrying the young girl and Charles supporting the boy, leaving the others free to ride behind and meet such pursuers as might come.

But none pursued.

"I think they will find a task on hand to care for the other prisoners the open dungeon door unloosed," Sir Galahad said.

"And with the wonder over Sir Dolphus," Sir Launcelot added and his look was far away.

A day later found them at the castle of Sanscourt. Happy was my Lady Jeanne over the return of her dear child-

ren and grateful, too. It did not take long for them to prepare to go forth to England with Sir Launcelot and Merlin.

So they bade each the other goodbye. And as they went forth, Sir Galahad watching them go, said to the Lady Jeanne.

"Still hope, my lady. For I shall bring or send you word of Sir Vilard, good or bad."

"I shall never cease to hope, Sir Galahad. And I shall pray for you, each day until you return."

[209]

CHAPTER TWENTY-NINE

# Facing the East

SO then the trio turned toward the East seeking but never finding that all elusive Grail which seemed ever ahead of them. Strange lands they passed through and it left them with wonderment at the bigness of the world in which they lived.

For Sir Galahad and for the boy Charles, each day brought the wonder of new things to see. For Walker, the Squire, though he would not make confession to his master, there grew the wish to see again the pleasant green of England's shore. None of the wonders of these strange lands held allure for him, since they but proved England's greater worth.

But when twitted by his master he would make no confession of his home-sickness.

"Nay master. I am a man and would hold it weak whimsy to let yearning for my home land encompass me. I go where you will and soon enough will I make return to our home shores."

And the Grail, Symbol of Honor, of Faith, of Service and of Piety! No nearer to the finding did the young knight ap-

pear to be. Even so, the zest for it, the need for finding it stayed ever with him.

So he reached Rome and stayed in it for many days. Many strangers were there from many lands but few who knew of the Holy Grail. And none who could tell him where it could be found.

"I would seek, were I you, in the Holy Land," said one pious man. While still another thought so holy a thing would never be permitted to go so far as England and that the knight's search was fruitless.

From Rome Sir Galahad went north to Lombardy in search of news of Sir Vilard. Long was his search here but not hopeless. Nor need we make record of how at last he found that the Gascon was not dead but imprisoned with some of the other knights of that ill fated group. And when ransom was agreed to he returned to Rome and sent a message to Sir Launcelot by a friendly English knight to find the Lady Jeanne and have sent to him the ransom desired.

Months passed. Then came Ambrose and with him the gold for the freedom of his father and his companions. So that they were free. Only then did Sir Galahad go on.

He reached the Holy Land in company with others, men who came there to pay reverence, men who came to repent of many sins, men who ever restless must journey everywhere. And on the way he had gained the friendship of an old priest whose journey he had made somewhat the lighter by such help as youth may offer old age.

The priest had been greatly interested in the mission of the knight. Many were his questions, of where Sir Galahad had traveled, how far he purposed to journey in his search.

"My journeys shall not cease, good father, until I have found the Grail. For so have I set my whole life that I may find it. And time counts not. Though I wish it could be found right soon for then may I turn my face to England." Since Sir Galahad had spoken of Yosalinde, the priest understood.

"What then, Sir Knight, makes you think you will find the Grail in far lands?" the priest asked.

"It must need be so, since were it nearer home it would have been found long since."

To which the priest made no answer.

Days later, when they were gathered about again he told

the story of Elam, the son of Anner, who had a great desire to gain wisdom and knowledge.

"So then, young friends, he started out to learn from all the founts of wisdom. Far he traveled and much he learned."

And then the reverend man gave long account of the places to which Elam had gone and the things he had learned. It was a tale of many years and it took time in the telling.

"Then when he had learned much of the wisdom of the then world and had gained in knowledge, he returned home. And when he was there but a few days, lo, he found that yet had his father Anner, greater knowledge than he and wisdom more profound. And he knew this now, returned home from all his sojournings. Nor would he have known this unless he had traveled far, for my sons, it was in this way that he gained the vision to see. Of a truth, it was then that he knew that his father was wisest of men and well could he learn from him."

"I have not heard of this man Elam, before," Sir Galahad said. "Yet had he great need to travel, if he gained this vision to see."

"True and well spoken, Sir Knight," replied the priest and watched him keenly.

## CHAPTER THIRTY

# Homeward

STILL further did Sir Galahad have a mind to travel but he found from learned men that to go further East was to travel into uncertainties which few had ventured before him. Nor would he have paused even then, were it not that he realized well that little likelihood was there for the Lost Grail to be found in the far East.

So he turned his face west again. Slowly he made his way home. There were days now, he misdoubted the success of his search and he questioned his own worthiness.

After months and months of travel he reached France once again. When he came to Gascony he found the rightful ruler on the throne and the house of Sanscourt, well and happy. Great was the welcome given the knight by the happy family and a great feast was held for them. The Lady Jeanne was radiant with the happiness which had returned after seeming desertion.

"We owe you much, Sir Galahad," said Sir Vilard, "so very much that it is beyond repayment."

"Mine and Sir Launcelot's was the joy of service, my lord. That you must well understand."

When they reached Normandy, Charles was given a happy reception. He had grown, and had profited well by his travels and service to Sir Galahad whom he would not leave now. For he hoped to be made a knight by him. In Normandy, Sir Galahad stayed for more than a month. He had acquired great fame because of his travels and deeds yet did he find small pleasure in this for the great purpose of his journeys had failed.

It was on a day just before he was to return to England. He had mounted the Seeker and without companion had gone forth for the morning. His thoughts were of the Grail, of his great wish to find it, and ever with his thoughts the wish to prove to Yosalinde that it was in him to find it. Well he knew that she would understand his desire even though he could not bring to her the fulfillment of that desire.

"Yet who am I to find myself disheartened. I must not question, keep ever seeking." So he thought to himself and gave no heed to where the Seeker carried him.

Nor did it seem strange to the knight that he found him-

self in a narrow path of the woods and before him the strange monk who had first given him urge to seek the Holy Grail.

"I greet you, holy father. Nor can I say to you that I have yet proven worthy of the finding of that which I have long sought."

"Yet have you traveled far, my son. Is it not so?"

"Far and to many lands, holy sir. But nowhere have I found that which brought me nearer to it."

"Too, I know how worthy of the finding you are. Well have you kept your purpose high, knightly have your deeds been?"

"Holy father, I have but tried. Ever have I kept your words before me. And deem it all worth the while, even though it end with my not finding the Grail. For, father, this will I always say, that joy has there been in the seeking."

"Think you then, my son, you will not find it?" the monk asked.

"I know not, father. Think me not grown tired of the search. Think not that I complain that the search is long or arduous. I shall go on seeking where the call may lead me.

And ever seek to be worthy of finding it. He who decides all things shall decide as to that. Nor will He find me ever questioning. For this I have found. God is good and His ways are ever for the best."

"Glad am I to hear that the search goes on. My blessing goes with you. Well have I kept the count of all the days of your journeyings and great is my pride in you. So son, seek on for who can tell what the morrow brings."

Then the holy man left him. Yet Sir Galahad did not go until long after sundown. And when he did, doubled was the strength of his purpose.

And on the morrow he was on his way to England.

[217]

## Chapter Thirty-One

# The Beggar and The Grail

ENGLAND to Charles, was indeed strange but so much had Walker spoken thereof that he looked forward to seeing it as if it were his native land. The joy of Walker at its nearness, though he tried to hide it under pretended calm was yet a thing quite obvious to Sir Galahad and the boy and much did it amuse them.

"Of all the fair lands we have passed through, have you yet found none that pleased you more, good Walker?" the knight asked him.

"There is but one heaven, my master and there is but one England," replied Walker.

"Then must I confess my sorrow at keeping you this long time from heaven," said his master with mock regret.

"Nay, master, one can only know heaven when one has seen all the other places. Too, I care not even for England when my master is not there."

"Kind words, good Walker. And spoke I ten times as kindly, yet could I not do justice to how much you have count-

ed and how well. Will I say this, that I find it sweet to know that we are so near to England's shores and that it is but a few days when we shall again find ourselves at home. I would see all our friends, the good king, Sir Percival, Sir Gareth, Sir Launcelot and the others. This wind that fills these sails cannot blow too strong for me.

Well did the wind hold yet did it seem as if the next days were over long. At last they were but a half day from the great castle of King Arthur.

Now as they rode, adventure there had been none since they had left Normandy, they were stopped by a strange beggar who sought alms. Sick did he seem, ragged and wretched, and as if life could hold but little for him. It was the selfsame beggar they had passed when they started on their journey.

"Good master, I starve. Charity I seek."

Now though, Sir Galahad was impatient to reach the castle, yet did he stop for the poor wretch drew his pity.

"What will you, my man?"

"Food, if you have it, Sir Knight. Such help as you can give so low a thing as me."

So then without further ado, he bade Walker feed the knave, which the latter did, grumbling at the delay the same

must cause. Then, the knight spoke kindly again to the beggar and gave him some silver.

"Master," the beggar said. "The Lord will bless you, for you found time for so wretched a soul as me. Far have you traveled, many of high degree have found it honor to hold speech with you. So great a knight as you and yet have you had time for the beggar on the road.

"Honor have you shown, Faith have you ever had. Service have you rendered. This day you prove that you have Piety and Charity. So then for your food and for your silver and your kind words and the spirit behind it all, I pay you now. Here, then is the Grail. Long sought in many lands, in many places, yet was it always near at home."

"The Grail? Here, where I never thought to see it. And a beggar to possess it. Aye, even the lowliest possesses riches."

Mixed were the knight's emotions nor could he voice the thoughts and the feelings within him. While nearby the two with him watched it all in awed silence.

"Aye, Sir Galahad. Think not that your search in far lands was fruitless. Rather was it the caldron in which your worth was seasoned. Yet will this fact ever remain—that one need not travel far to find Honor, Faith, Service and Piety. For these are ever near."

"I am like Elam who went everywhere and found that what he sought was near at home."

"True, good knight. This day shall be a great day for England, for through the worth of one of its knights, the Grail stays here. Go you then, for word will already be at the Round Table that Sir Galahad comes with the Grail."

"Strange man, I know not what to say. Dear is the possession of this precious vessel to me. Long have I sought it. And to find it to have been so near at home stirs mixed and wondrous feelings within me. So I can but go and if I fail to say the thing I should, forgive me."

The knight, Charles and Walker as well, found themselves kneeling to receive the benediction of this strange man who was both beggar and holy man. And when they looked up again he was gone.

"Thought I," said Walker, "that that day, my master found this Grail there would be great doings, that there would be great combats. Instead of which a seeming beggar has it to give us. Verily, it is far beyond me."

And the good squire scratched his head in great puzzlement.

## CHAPTER THIRTY-TWO

# Conclusion

WE find our story now near ended. We can well see the great welcome given the still youthful knight as he entered the great hall. There was King Arthur in high good humor. About him stoo' many of the knights of the Round Table, and among them Sir Galahad saw his many friends. And as the young knight stood there there came to him the memory of that first day and the wondrous hope he had had now come true.

In all the hall none was so happy as that brave and noble hearted knight, Sir Launcelot. Well pleased he was. Merlin was there, also well content. And there, when they sat down to the great feast spread out for them, Sir Galahad told the story of his search or the Grail. A long tale it was for they would hear it all. To it they listened in silence, without interruption, until he had done.

Though he showed it not, the young knight was eager to be free of all these friends. For he had great desire to hasten

to the home of Sir Percival.   He knew from what Sir Percival told him, Yosalinde would be there.   Yet could he not leave until the late afternoon.

Swiftly did the Seeker take him there.   Eagerly he sought the sight of the castle as if in seeing that, he would also see this damsel who had helped so much to give him the great purpose of his search.   But it was not until he had entered within, that he saw her.

So we draw the curtain and leave you to suppose the joy and the gladness of this welcome.   And though to each the finding of the Holy Grail was of high importance yet they spoke not of that but of other things for many an hour until the sun had gone down and darkness had come.

Wonderful was the picture Sir Galahad had carried of his lady, yet he found the real presence far dearer.   Of the things they talked, one was the future and what it meant to both of them.

We leave them then.   High the moon shines, the stars are everywhere.   It is a wonderful night, soft the gentle breeze. Such a night as each had pictured for their first meeting.

[223]

Charles, the Norman lad, had his wish come true in good time, when Sir Galahad made him a knight. Then the new knight made his way back to Normandy. It was his children's children who made their way in later days to England and settled there.

The deeds of the brave knights of the Round Table continued great and glorious. Sir Galahad, Sir Launcelot, Sir Percival and the others upheld the honor of King Arthur's court. And never did Sir Galahad lower the banner of his great house.

**Honor, Faith, Service and Piety.**